"Ancient technologies, forgotten magic, and pirates in a plot that is a mix of old and new weird fiction. What's not to love? A tour de force equivalent of a trilogy in the length of a novella... gripping and intriguing. Carmelo Rafala does a fine job of delivering a narrative with a flavor reminiscent of Fritz Leiber and Sarah Monette, with a sprinkle of Kurosawa (think *Rashomon*)."

—Fábio Fernandes, author of *Under Pressure*

"Carmelo Rafala's *The Madness of Pursuit* is not only a swashbuckling adventure on an alien sea, it's also an affecting story with a haunting mystery at its core. Superb world-building and complex characters make for a riveting read!"

—Mercurio D. Rivera, author of *Across the Event Horizon*

"A ravishing tale filled with wonder and surprise set on a dreamy word of oceans and islands. There is beauty in the writing and passion in the plot... but not everything is quite what it seems on the surface: there are darker currents bubbling beneath. A fabulous fantasy, a tangled web of truths, mysteries and revelations."

—Rhys Hughes, author of *Better the Devil* and *Worming the Harpy, and Other Bitter Pills*

The MADNESS of PURSUIT

Carmelo Rafala

GUARDBRIDGE BOOKS
ST ANDREWS, SCOTLAND

Published by Guardbridge Books,
St Andrews, Fife, United Kingdom.

http://guardbridgebooks.co.uk

The Madness of Pursuit

© 2020 by Carmelo Rafala. All rights reserved.

No part of this book may be reproduced in any written, electronic, recording, or photocopying manner without written permission of the publisher or author.

This is a work of fiction. All characters and events portrayed in this book are fictitious, and any resemblance to real people or events is purely coincidental.

Cover art by Victor Ferraz.

ISBN: 978-1-911486-49-7

A special thanks to Cynthia Ward
for her encouragement, and for reading
and critiquing the first draft.

CONTENTS

a veil of white foam 1

PART ONE 5

old photographs 31

PART TWO 33

a loose pane of glass.................. 71

PART THREE 75

of burning tears and bright water 107

a veil of white foam

Through the window I can see the breakers roll in. They hiss and crash against the rocks, disintegrate in a veil of white foam, run back out, and tumble in again. A storm approaches across the evening sea.

Fortune kept my ship one step ahead of its fury. If I complete my task, if I make it home, I will give thanks in the Temple of Isa—something I have not done since I was a boy.

But then, over the long years, I've had very little to be thankful for.

I hear footsteps and the archive's Director reappears from behind a stack of files, carrying two texts. He is a wisp of a man and walks with his shoulders bent forward, as though the two books comprise a great burden. Though at first his appearances may give the impression he is older than his years, I can see in his face the remnants of a man younger than myself.

He places a volume on the desk near me. I scan the gold words on the cover:

> **Excerpts from eye-witness accounts taken from the annals of Avram Aul, record keeper and advisor to the Magistrate of the Islands of Quiru.**
> **LEVEL FIVE.**

"A government text, Director?"

"I authorize you to read it." He notices my frown. "There is no deception here. Members of the public may access Level Five classifications at my discretion, such is my authority. Be satisfied."

"But I'm a stranger from a distant island—"

"Yes, I recognised the top-knot of Sengalor." He tilts his head. "Much has changed over the years. Our new Magistrate has been generous in downgrading certain texts for the public."

I open the book. The leaves are crisp yet stained with time. *Is she in here?* I wonder.

When I look up, he misinterprets my expression.

"You said you wished to develop the most complete image of the fugitive Dema Ägan and her J'Niah companion, Rymah," he says.

"My people know very little of these waters and hear few of your stories. We are aware of Dema Ägan, but nothing detailed."

He nods at the emblem on my golden sash. "Did the Duke not send you to track her down? Forgive me, but you do not look like a bounty hunter."

I breathe deep. "I was Midshipman aboard the *Morning Star*. We were hired out to the Duke's Export Company to establish new trade routes."

"You *were* Midshipman, but no longer?"

"I bought out the remaining time on my contract, got off at the Nawa'i Atoll and made my way here." I lock eyes with him. "As I said, we know very little of these waters."

"Then your interest in the matter of Dema Ägan is simple curiosity?"

"Yes," I lie.

A shadow crosses his face. "Sengalor is far from Quiru, but you are not from Sengalor. You are from farther still, I think."

My accent must have slipped through on a word or particular phrasing. I throw my shoulders back. "Does it matter?"

He considers me for a moment, uncertain of something, then says: "It does not."

Silence grows up between us. Upon the shore, the waves shatter like glass.

"Well," he says stiffly, "if you were a bounty hunter you would not have been the first, though you're the first to inquire after Dema Ägan in many years. The price on her head is still active, though she's no longer considered a person of priority."

Oh, but she *is* a person of priority. She is *my* priority. And I need to know if she is really the person the stories say; I need to know what really happened, and why. I need to find her and satisfy my hate.

I return the man's gaze blandly. "I'll need other sources."

"Of course." He places the second book on the desk, carefully, as though it is made of crystal. "I recommend you begin with this particular account. Although not a complete record, it offers a unique perspective."

> **The story of Dema Ägan—**
> **mariner, criminal,**
> **Mistress Captain of the *Sceptre of Night*,**
> **as written by Rainer Eicher,**
> **dramatist of island folklore.**

"Rainer Eicher." I frown. "This name means nothing to me."

"Why would it? This play was not widely circulated even among these islands."

"A dramatist." I grunt my dissatisfaction. "Does this not suggest an extreme interpretation of events?"

He shrugs. "It's a story seldom told, of Dema and Rymah, and the boy Selasi, and It's Eicher's definitive text. Indeed, I have verified it to be a precise copy of the lost original."

I raise an eyebrow. "And how did you verify this?"

"I am the last to have read the original manuscript, before the fire destroyed the library at Kulain. I was a young lad then, cheeky and full of vinegar." His lips quiver slightly. "But I remember every word."

Warily I touch the brown leather covering; doubt pools in the tips of my fingers.

"I trust you will find what you are looking for." He departs.

A gust rattles the window. I sit in the chair at the desk and place my hand firmly upon Eicher's book. That face returns to me out of the night—her face—to prickle my flesh and freeze my heart.

I breathe deep, open Eicher's book, turn a page, and begin to read.

PART ONE

In which Dema Ägan, quest-captain and fugitive,
finds herself stranded on the isle of Tanpai,
and of the strange offer made to her there…

ONE

–From the narrative by Rainer Eicher

Dema pulled in her nets when she spotted the black ships. From a raised dais on the tall, ancient machine where she had spent the night fishing for artefacts, she caught Rymah's attention with a frantic gesture of arms and hands.

See them! Yes, Rymah signed back.

Flotation outriggers bumped the towering, faux-metallic stalk of the ancient machine as their navigator secured the ship. "Make ready!" Dema yelled down to him. "We may cut it close!" She spun round and pulled herself up the nearest hanging cable to the next flower-like platform while Rymah, six levels above, scurried across swaying walkways.

Calm down, Dema signed up to her, *and unhook the pole!*

"What are you doing?" the navigator asked.

"If I can get the pole attachment," Dema said, "the winch can haul in the nets. We need those artefacts, and this particular field of machines have sloughed off more parts than usual this time of year."

Gunshots rattled the air.

"Forget the other nets," said the Navigator. "we've got to go now!"

Dema signed *Get moving!* but her J'Niah companion offered no response and flittered on, like a bird in a cage. Dema bit her lip and glanced about at the still silent machines. She realised Rymah's agitated state had little to do with the approaching ships, and more to do with the menacing stalks towering around them.

Thunder cracked like a whip and the machine-stalk shuddered.

She gripped the pendant hanging between her breasts, felt its smooth coolness through her shirt. Rymah had given it to her not long after they had been reunited, not long after Captain Meloy had been found in a pool of his own blood and shit. The pendant was a token of Rymah's trust, her belief that Dema would protect her, cherish her, and prove her devotion by taking up the quest.

She had performed two-thirds of her commission with equal skill. But running from the law, avoiding bounty hunters, Dema had little time for mythical cities such as Anua, or stories of Lost Years.

And now, black ships.

She knew the risks when she had steered the *Sceptre of Night* this far out. But they were low on supplies and money. She had hoped for a moment's good fortune; that's all she needed, to sail in quietly to some foreign port with a haul of artefacts, maybe strike it rich—

"Now!" said the navigator. "Let's go!" He stood with a long knife in his hand, ready to cut the nets.

Dema gripped one of the many cables hanging down from the machine, leaned back and craned her neck. "Rymah!"

To the east, the two black vessels of the Karahsek Dominion cut through the sea, the sound of their engines growing louder.

"A few minutes more," she mumbled, watching the ships approach. "Just a few minutes…"

Gunshots again.

"Mistress Captain, we've got to leave!" The Navigator's voice was strained.

"Hold your position." Dema pulled the rifle out from her back holster, rounded the stalk and returned fire. Before she could change cartridges, the machine's sea-stalk began to glow and tremble; a whining noise burned through her skull. The other ancient sea-stalks joined in, glowing, droning.

The net-lines slackened; the pole attachment came sliding down the makeshift guideline. Sparing one hand she caught it and leaned over the edge to yell, "Be ready to cast off!" but a slug caught her navigator in the head. He twisted and fell into the water.

The waters around the machines began to froth and turn over. She looked up to see the black ships quickly backing off, making a run for the open sea.

A new frequency pierced her skull. Dema fell to her knees and, dropping the rifle, gritted her teeth and covered her ears.

Rymah was now beside her. In one swift motion she encircled Dema with her arms and threw them both over the edge of the platform. They crashed onto the decking of the ship below, just inches from the wheel.

Skull filled with fire, Dema managed to reach up and palm the displacement device on the steering column just as the stalks of the machines shuddered and burst to life, discharging their gathered energies into the sky.

TWO

–From the narrative by Rainer Eicher

With tattered sun-sails, burned patches of hull and blown electrics, they were forced to dock at the island realm of Tanpai—a small isolated chain of islands as far from the Confederate Archipelago as possible without passing the borders of known civilisation. Despite the great distance between the island and the Confederacy, the port town of Onolu was anything but the wretched dive she was expecting. The harbour was well-kept and modern; the houses tall and straight, and it seemed as though the spires behind them, rising out of the town centre, were formed of some iridescent crystal.

Dema Ägan's bloodied and burned flesh did little to endear her to the crowd that gathered as they stepped off the gangplank. She noticed how Rymah kept her brilliant yellow eyes fixed upon the cobbled walk, noticed how she seemed to quake ever so slightly. The sheen of Rymah's dark hair, black as night, reflected the noonday sun in sparkles like crisp stars.

At any other time, such a picture of beauty would have made Dema feel warm. Not now. Not with injuries, a crippled vessel, and the eyes of a foreign mob pressing in upon them.

Dema's fingers tapped the grip of the gun sheathed on her thigh. It was time to act the part she had created for herself.

"You!" She pointed at a boy in the crowd. "What do they call you?"

"Mistress Captain," he said, bowing respectfully, brown ponytail bobbing at the back of his head. "I am called Selasi. A bard by trade." He bowed again.

"I have no need for a bard. Where's the dock officer?"

"Mistress Captain, no one is expected at this mooring." The boy's eyes, grey like ash, shifted to Rymah, and lingered there.

And with that Dema noticed the mutterings, the sideways glances, as though Rymah were a curiosity escaped from a circus.

"Something wrong, young Selasi?"

"Apologies, Mistress Captain," the boy said, eyes locked on Rymah, "I mean no disrespect. We rarely see J'Niah in Tanpai—"

Dema pushed a finger into his shoulder. "Look at me when I speak to you."

"Yes, Mistress Captain."

"Find the dock officer," she said. "Tell him the *Sceptre of Night* has arrived, and graciously seeks the shelter of this harbour."

"Shelter?" he echoed, mulling the word over. He spat over the side of the jetty. "*Protection* will cost more—" He stole a quick glance at Rymah. "Are you a quest-captain?"

"What I am is of no consequence when the officer realises what's out there."

"And what is out there?" A path formed through the crowd. The officer appeared, clad in a long coat made of brown leather squares. A silver badge glinted from the breast. Three armed guards followed.

She bowed. "Sir, I am Dema Ägan, Captain of the *Sceptre of Night*. Under oath to the Proprietor of the

Confederate Archipelago, it is my duty to report an attempted act of piracy."

"Black ships," someone muttered.

The officer regarded her. "The black ships of the Karahsek have not plagued our waters since the Regent declared Tanpai a neutral realm. *You*, on the other hand, land without flag, without permission, and at a mooring not scheduled for use today; it also appears" –he looked her up and down, at the blood and burns sprawled across her exposed flesh— "that you've narrowly escaped a purging of the great sea-machines. Well, shelter is not easily forthcoming to novices who spin outlandish tales."

"Do not take me for a fool. I spin no tales. And I'm no novice."

"Novice or fool, they are much the same." He motioned to a guard, who ran up the gangplank and disappeared into the ship's hold. "I'm Officer Kerrod," he continued, "and you're far from the Confederacy."

"According to my charts," Dema said, "that sea-field to the north sits on the edge of your territory. Those Karahsek ships may not enter into your waters, but they play fast and loose with the border—"

"We don't often see Confederate ships out here. Why are you so far from your usual trade routes?" Kerrod did not wait for a response. "What is the condition of your vessel?"

"Two of our sun-sails need replacing, the electronics board has short-circuited and one of our six battery cells is completely burnt out."

"Crew?"

"One navigator. Lost at sea."

"And?"

"That's all," she said.

He fixed her with a stony glare. "It's unusual to travel without a bard," he said, "especially if you're a quest-captain. Are you? A quest-captain?"

Before she could respond the guard had returned from the *Sceptre*. He handed Kerrod a small item, one of the many trinkets Dema had fished from the waters around the machines.

"You will fill out a statement when you are fit enough, Mistress Captain," he said, studying the item. "In the meantime, I'm impounding your ship."

Fear rippled through her, but her poise remained authoritative and her voice held the practiced tone of deliberate offense: "I can pay the docking charge, and for the repairs to my ship."

"No, Mistress Captain. I don't think you can."

"If you allow me the privilege of accessing your markets—"

"Denied." Kerrod now eyed Rymah, as though for the first time. "You see, we don't deal in machine artefacts, so we have no need for the services a J'Niah may offer." Kerrod pointed to the boy, Selasi. "*You!* Get some men and confiscate any cargo aboard."

The boy cast a nervous glance at Dema. "Apologies, Mistress Captain," he said, pushed through the crowd, and ran down the dock.

Dema wondered if her own nerves were showing. She threw her shoulders back. "Does Tanpai's neutrality forsake the mariner's code of hospitality?"

"You will be cared for." Kerrod held the piece up. "And I will authorize repairs. But the cost, as well as the dock charge, will be considerable. Unless you can find a way to pay your debts, I will release your ship to anyone who can cover the expense. That is Tanpai law." Kerrod motioned to the guards: "Disarm the captain and take her to medical."

Dema knew arguing would be futile. Kerrod was doing his job. And Misfortune had done hers.

"My ship," she said. "I expect only skilled technicians will touch her. We have standards in the Confederacy."

Kerrod raised an eyebrow. "Undoubtedly." He placed both hands behind his back. "Anything else?"

The crowd was still there, still muttering.

Rymah pushed into her, seeking reassurance.

"Will she be safe?" Dema said.

Kerrod regarded Rymah with cold indifference.

"It's not illegal for her to be here," he said, and then turned on his heel and disappeared into the crowd.

THREE

The account of Jan Kakhidze, dock master of Sola Din, port of Quiru.
–From the annals of Avram Aul

When her name first became known in the taverns of Quiru, Dema Ägan was Boatswain of the *Wayfarer*. Ship's captain, Tove Garbarek, put into port for crew replacements and electrical repairs. One man had been lost in a storm; three others shot down in a skirmish with black ships.

The *Wayfarer* was a majestic vessel, boasting three grand masts, nine sun-sails, and flying the silver and maroon banners of the Islands of Gish. Although her sides were riddled with bullet marks, the sheer elegance of her carved woodwork remained mostly unscathed; her sweeping designs the work of master craftsmen found only among the peoples of those far islands.

Dema could be seen on the foredeck as the mariners crowded the dock to watch the *Wayfarer,* that beauty of the sea, slide gracefully into the harbour, her pride still very much intact.

The ship had been secured and dock charges paid. As standard practice—and in the interest of good relations for the fostering of trade—we stationed two guards at her berth to watch over the vessel. Garbarek issued leave for the rest of the crew, as they would not be required until the repairs had been completed.

Dema had no intention of staying in Quiru, nor do I think she would have been welcomed to do so. You see, she spent her first night in a holding cell. She had been charged with inciting violence in the *Hope and Ruin* tavern. Dema was certainly handy in a bar fight, and she proceeded to demonstrate her skills on more than one occasion, until she was banned from three of our finest establishments.

Ships had always been her home, she stated, since the age of thirteen, and while she enjoyed the warmth of soil and rock under her feet the feeling was often short-lived. She would soon be itching to get back out upon the open water, where the rambling wind and driving currents stirred her restless blood.

And then she met Captain Meloy.

And his J'Niah woman.

FOUR

–From the narrative by Rainer Eicher

They were given a room in a public house, courtesy of the local Authority. Not so much an inn as a sparsely furnished cell, Dema thought, a fit place for wayward mariners who posed a financial risk.

She was treated by the harbour doctor, and then a guard took them to their room. He threw the keys on a table and departed, closing the door behind him.

Rymah sat on the edge of the bed, her frame silhouetted against the window. The room was painted in pastel hues by the dusky light of the waning day. Dema sank into the mattress like a collapsing sail.

Rymah signed: *To sea we go. How long?*

"I don't know," Dema vocalised. Her scalded flesh, soothed by a doctor's balms, pulsed mildly beneath their dressings. *Let's not lose our nerve,* she signed. *The ship is safe, at least. We'll get the* Sceptre *back.*

Rymah did not seem convinced. *How will you do this?*

Although artefacts fallen from the stalks of the great machines fetched a good price—particularly those which induced visions or healed some ailment—they were contraband in Tanpai, and they had little else with which to barter.

Tomorrow, Dema would have to go to the markets and buy food with what little coin they had. The Authority were housing them, not feeding them.

I'll score some work, Dema signed, *maybe as a dockhand. I can keep an eye on the* Sceptre. *If she goes out under new command, we can charter a ship to catch her up. Remember,* Dema held up a palm, *the* Sceptre *won't get far. I've stolen back that ship once before, if you recall, from that fool, Lonigan. If needs be, I can steal it again.*

The look in Rymah's eyes spoke of uncertainty, an insecurity that for so long had characterised their lives together.

The madness of the last eighteen months gnawed at Dema's bones. However, there was some small consolation in the fact that she had put almost half a world between them and the Islands of Quiru.

She had to stay strong for Rymah's sake. For her own sake. They had been running too hard and for too long. And without result. The city of Anua—and the safety Rymah believed it offered—seemed no closer now than when they had first started out. And why should it? After all, Anua was a fabled place no one had ever seen. It was whimsy, a half-forgotten dream.

But Dema was very much awake, and she had little time to entertain such folly. She was too busy keeping them alive.

Dema also knew she could not allow herself to openly criticize Rymah's convictions too often. Dema was no stranger to confrontation and was often the victim of her inability to control her belligerent nature. But she hated it when they fought; it unnerved her. It was much easier to allow Rymah to indulge in the comfort of her beliefs.

The J'Niahs were, after all, an unusual people. Mystical, nomadic, they were often thought of as sorcerers of a forgotten magic. This was particularly prevalent where the giant sea-machines were concerned.

As though driven by some peculiar affinity with the machines Rymah, like all J'Niahs, could not only interpret the purpose of various artefacts that fell from the ancient structures but also knew how to make them work.

And Dema came to understand that Rymah possessed an awareness that seemed to go beyond thought, a capacity to feel so deeply that it penetrated to the essence of Dema's being. Rymah had reached into her and stirred something to life, something Dema did not want to let die. A need. A desire. A passion. But for what, exactly, she did not know. All she knew was that she needed Rymah.

And Rymah needed her.

The J'Niah's soft yellow eyes, exotic and otherworldly, penetrated the near darkness. She reached over, fingers moving slowly up Dema's body. Dema shivered with anticipation. Rymah's long, thin fingers stopped at the pendant hanging between Dema's breasts.

Rymah gripped the pendant and removed the artefact from around Dema's neck. It's reflective surface, smooth and circular, shed sparks as her fingers brushed over the faux metal, reading its unseen language as only a J'Niah knew how. The sparks engaged themselves in an alien dance and coalesced, splinter by splinter, until the outline of a magnificent city grew up from Rymah's palm. Anua. The city of light.

Or so Dema had been told.

Rymah sighed heavily, and in that moment Dema's own heart seemed overcome with emotion. It was a shared intensity like no other, a desire that threatened to swallow her whole.

And although she felt Rymah's yearning, the compulsion for Anua that plagued the minds and souls of the J'Niah, it was not the desire Dema, at that moment, wanted to partake in. She pushed the fantasy away, as she had done so many times before.

We go, Rymah gestured. *To Anua.*

"I know." Dema pushed herself up on her elbows, put her hand through the image, and lay her palm over the pendant. The city vanished.

Rymah placed the pendant on the nightstand.

"This is not the first time we've run into difficulty, Rymah, is it? And it won't be the last, either. But if we're going to make it, we've got to keep our heads. And stick together."

Rymah's face was now framed by a painful disquiet.

"We're safe for the moment," Dema said. "Black ships won't land here."

Rymah remained still and said nothing.

Dema reached across the sheets to take her hand, but Rymah folded her arms.

"I'll walk with sharp ears, as always." Dema slid closer to her. "If the *Godsong* is about, I'll know. Captain Ogunwe won't gain an advantage over us again." Dema flicked a lock of hair away from Rymah's cheek. "I promise. I made a mistake then, and it almost cost us. But we've made it this far—"

Rymah turned her whole body away from her and faced the window, eyes fixed out to the darkening sea.

FIVE

The account of Minghella Lang, immigrant to the island nation of Quiru *and owner of* The Blue Mariner.
–From the annals of Avram Aul

Captain Meloy had been held up in Quiru for weeks, awaiting repairs to his ship. With very little money and nothing left to barter, he was forced to rent a dingy little room in the seaside village of Korum, three kilometres down the shoreline. He walked up to Sola Din every day and took odd jobs around the dockyards to help pay for the maintenance. He spent most of his evenings at the *The Blue Mariner* on the quay, and as a quest-captain he endured his fair share of ridicule from the other mariners.

Although it was known—or rather he claimed—he had spent all his life at sea, the woman Dema Ägan commented she thought him more an entertainer than a seasoned mariner. Who can disagree? After all, it must be stated that his voice was, indeed, as magnetic as a trained thespian, and he possessed the shrewd, intimate gaze of the practiced performer.

Face loaded with contempt, she listened to him tell outrageous stories of outrunning black ships, surviving the great storm season, even navigating parts of the Uncharted Seas to the Deep West…these are the stories quest-captains are made of.

And she laughed and poured scorn on him, as did the other mariners. But like the others she always came back for another lurid, impossible tale. (Despite her reputation for violence, she caused no trouble here. She could be brusque, argumentative, of course, but she certainly did not seem the kind to commit the crimes of which she stands accused. But I digress…)

One night, Dema sat with him at a table in a corner of the room not far from the bar. The table was lit by a single oil lamp hanging down from the rafters. The J'Niah woman sat in the shadows next to Meloy, silent, unmoving. It was as though she were but a slip of a ghost.

"Anua is there," Meloy said, leaning forward. "At the heart of the marshland continent, in the Uncharted Seas of the Deep West."

"All this from the mouth of a half-crazed mariner you found drifting in a skiff near the Uncharted Seas? You'll have to do better than *that.*"

He threw himself back into his chair. "The tale of Jorunn tells us it can be reached. She sailed her ship into the Uncharted Seas on a dare—"

"—and landed there. Or so the story goes. And how long did she sail before sighting land? Even Jorunn couldn't say, and her ship's log was lost, and we only have the ship's bard's account to go by. But they were out there long enough for equipment to begin malfunctioning. Ship's water was almost putrid, food stores near empty—"

"—but she made it!"

"She failed to return to her ship. In the story she took two crewmen and tried to navigate the skiff inland through a maze of winding channels. The first mate waited as long as he could, then after replenishing their supplies with what he could find, he gave the order to put out to open water. Somehow, they managed to find their way back." Dema shook her head. "Anua is a fable, and a killing fable at that."

"I can find it! The marshland, and Anua. Just as sure as I know the ancient Anil built the many sea-fields of machines to prop up the sky!"

She snorted. "Without charts? And on the word of a wreck survivor and an old bard's story that contains no navigational information? Not likely. And I've *seen* your ship!"

Meloy's face became hard, and his eyes seemed to want to betray some deep secret.

"No, you haven't," he said, almost to himself. "Not *really*."

"You and I both know why those seas are uncharted. We all do. A compass is useless there." She drew a circle in the air with her finger. "The needle spins about. Can't navigate by the stars, either; they say that sea is domed by another sky."

"Unlike Jorunn, who sailed without the benefit of a J'Niah, I have *her*," he said, and twirled a strand of the J'Niah's hair between his fingers. "They have very peculiar gifts. Unfortunate their numbers have dwindled so."

The J'Niah woman's piercing yellow eyes glanced up at her for the first time. To most of us in the tavern that night, it appeared that Dema struggled to break free of the woman's gaze. It seemed as though something unspoken passed between them.

It is said they have a strange power and anyone who sees a J'Niah cannot help but be captivated by their looks—the high cheekbones, tapered chin, the warm glow of soft, smooth skin, and hair so black it shimmers with reflected light. And, of course, the eyes, small bright suns that stun the observer with their brilliance.

When Dema finally spoke, she said: "If it were that simple, some quest-captain would've found this Anua long ago."

"Perhaps," Meloy said, and became even more insistent that he could do it, although he stopped short of telling us all how.

And Dema Ägan? Truthfully, at that point she seemed more interested in his exotic companion than in hearing of his quest to find a fabled city.

Despite the many things we do not know about them—and despite how many feel the need to shun them—I believe the J'Niah are an intelligent, thinking, *feeling* people. And in that regard they are, in many ways, not to dissimilar to us.

SIX

–From the narrative by Rainer Eicher

The markets of this port town smelled of foods and spices and sweat. Electric trams rattled along their shining rails, decorated with the colourful dress of the affluent, who did not walk the cobbled streets at length, except to parade themselves around the high streets and market squares.

It was not unlike home, Dema thought. Busy. Crowded. And now anxious. Her arrival and her story of black ships near their waters had set the townspeople on edge. Most people ignored her, however, no doubt due to the presence of her J'Niah companion.

Leaving Rymah back in their room, Dema walked the mile-long bazaar day after day, buying little. She had gone down to the docks every morning as well, but there was no work. And each time, Kerrod was unavailable.

Turning the few coins left in her hand, she knew it was a matter of days before she was left begging for scraps. And the only way to get the ship back was to pay the charges.

She had to try the docks again. It was her only option.

Dema pulled her scarf over her mouth and dashed off. She had not learned to navigate her way around this port city, and what she assumed would be the quickest route back to the docks took her down narrow, winding alleyways, past gutted buildings of crumbling stone, choked with the squalor of poverty and neglect.

Someone moved in the shadows.

"Who's there?"

A figure came into the light. "Mistress Captain."

"Selasi?" she said.

"I often take this route home," he said quickly.

"Well, then, it is rather fortuitous that I've come across you. I could use your help."

He smiled. "Lost, Mistress?"

"You could say that. I'm looking for the docks."

"You are not far." He pointed down a darkening street, narrow and cobbled and smelling of urine. "But that way is the faster route."

"Thank you, young Selasi."

He stood, stiff, somber, then bowed and said, "Your servant, Mistress", and disappeared into the shadows.

She ducked under clothes lines, stepped over empty crates, ignoring the glances of the few prostitutes that lingered in doorways or under shadowed archways. Children sat around fires that burned in steel drums; they gazed at her with vacant eyes.

And then she noticed someone was blocking her way. A hand came toward her, palm up. "Mistress, if you please." The figure before her was wrapped in rags.

"*Unclean!*" cried a woman. People backed into buildings or scuttled down alleys; the children had disappeared.

Dema frowned. "Step aside, leper."

"Have mercy. Spare a coin."

"Out of my way." She had kept a baton up the sleeve of her long coat, and now let it slide down into her grip. The action did not go unnoticed.

The figure lunged at her, brought its other hand up and shoved it under her nose. She did not have time to react; the scent of whatever the creature held between its fingers was potent, and her paralysis was immediate. Her brain swam, vision blurred, and consciousness fell away.

She awoke in a room plagued by shadows. One dim gas lamp hung from a low ceiling. The wooden deck beneath her gently pitched and rolled to the cadence of the sea.

With that realisation she tried to spring up, only to find her hands tied behind her back. She thumped back down onto the planks. Her skull throbbed with its own dissonant rhythm.

"A holding platform," came Kerrod's voice, "not a ship." She could see him to her left. "I've heard you wanted to see me. About a job." He leaned over her. "I may have something for you. But first, I'm confused by one aspect of your statement, *Captain*."

"Really? Which part? I'll be sure and explain the big words to you."

"You say you trade up and down the island seas. But your ship is small, built for speed, and cannot hold enough cargo to make longer journeys profitable."

She looked through him, as though into a void. "Is that so?"

"You cannot possibly survive on the high seas. Food holds wouldn't last a season's turning."

"One learns to eat light—"

"And fitted weapons? The *Sceptre* is not built to carry them. How do you defend yourself?"

"Let's just say I'm an expert at running away."

He considered her words. "And yet you purposefully held your vessel in a sea-field of machines, on a build-up to a mass purging, for the sake of a few artefacts." He raised an eyebrow. "Why?"

Dema shrugged. "I eat light. But I do like to eat."

"Those black ships must've come up on you pretty fast."

"Fast enough," she said. "But they didn't hang around for long."

"True. But anyone with sense would steer clear of the machines when they are about to discharge. The timing required..." He shook his head. "Your survival is miraculous."

"So, you admit they were black ships," she said.

He took out a small device, placed it to her arm, and pulled the trigger. Currents of searing pain engulfed her. "Dema Ägan. I'll wager that's not your real name. What should I call you?"

She gasped. "You may call me *Mistress Captain*."

"Don't think to make a fool of me!"

"Novice or fool—" she began to say, and he pulled the trigger again. The pain tore through her in strips of white heat.

"Wanted for the murder of Captain Meloy and the unlawful appropriation of his vessel, formerly the *Wave Rider*. Yes, we hear things," Kerrod said, "even out here on the fringes."

"Hear things?" she replied, voice rasping. "Makes sense. Reading must be difficult for you."

He punched her in the mouth.

"You took flight from the Islands of Quiru. Months

later, a ship matching the *Wave Rider*'s description shows up in the Nawa'i Atoll with a Confederate registration number. Yes, my associates have had their eyes on you, *Captain* Ägan."

Associates? It was obvious Kerrod was not interested in the bounty on her head.

But he had the *Sceptre*.

And probably Rymah.

She suspected Tanpai's neutrality with the Karahsek came with a price. But what was for sale? If she played along, it was possible that arrangements would be made, fees somehow paid, documents signed, and her ship released...

Kerrod would make everything look legitimate. The Authority wouldn't notice any eccentricities in the details. She reasoned they wouldn't be looking for any. Why would they? Kerrod was their top officer.

"Find anything of interest in the sea-fields?" he continued. "Those ancient towers give up any secrets, my dear captain?"

Dema spat blood.

"What's that device under the wheel of your ship?" he asked.

"You noticed? Never did blend in with the decor."

"I suppose," he continued, "the apparatus to shift a vessel great distances—*if* it existed—would come from the machines of the Anil, from artefacts acquired by the able skills of a J'Niah."

"It might."

"Would make a ship worth stealing."

"Yes." Dema looked him in the eye. "I believe it would."

"That device would explain how a fugitive could evade capture for so long."

She nodded. "It's possible."

"Works with the touch of a hand. In fact," —He reached behind her, gripped her hand and squeezed it— "I bet the J'Niah somehow tuned that device, so it only responds to *your* hand. Is that something she could do for me? Would she want to?"

"She told me it can only be done twice."

"Of course," he said. "Meloy was the first. You're the second." He raised his eyebrows. "Don't look so surprised that I believe you. I have some knowledge of J'Niahs. When it comes to artefacts, they don't make mistakes."

She swallowed back the iron taste of blood. "So, what now?"

"Well, I won't kill you, unless you give me no choice. That would render your ship useless to me. No. You must continue to be a quest-captain in search of the lost city of Anua, inspired by the grandeur of a forgotten people." He moved to within a hair's breadth of her face. "So, what inspires your heart to the quest, *Mistress Captain*? The hidden knowledge of the Anil? The untold riches of a lost age? Or is it glory you seek?"

"Glory? Oh no, I've got plenty of that," she said. "Between my legs."

He shocked her again, this time for much longer.

"Now," he said, while she sputtered for breath, "shall we talk about that job?"

old photographs

I hold the page between my fingers but stop short of turning over; my mind is crowded with competing visions. There are none of the familiar tales here. No stories of brutal executions or premeditated murder. This story seems smaller, more personal. And the eyewitness accounts somehow compliment what I've read thus far.

I bookmark my page, pick up Avram's text, and flip to the appendix at the back. Old photographs live there. Rough black and white images, edges tainted yellow. I finger my way through them. Faces slide past me. The eyewitnesses. Tove Garbarek. Captain Meloy.

And the woman who called herself Dema Ägan.

I grow cold, a bitter, polar cold, and the hairs on the back on my neck stand up.

A scruffy, weather-eaten coat hangs off her shoulders. High, prominent cheekbones. Cracked and calloused lips slightly parted. Hair, wavy and unkempt, dangling just below her ears. And her eyes. They are wide and dull and empty, like the eyes of a corpse.

I run my finger along the edges of the photograph. I feel the blood rush in my ears. It has been many years, many long years, but it is her. I remember those eyes, that vacant look.

And I remember the terrible thing she did to me.

In the caption below the author declares this to be the only surviving photograph of Dema Ägan, taken at the port medical facilities in Tanpai not long after the *Sceptre of Night* landed there.

Dema Ägan. Mariner. Once part of a vast ship and crew, and later a fugitive and lone trader. Ragged. Destitute. Living a hand-to-mouth existence.

And the only thing she seemed to covet, besides her stolen vessel, was Rymah.

I look back through the pictures.

But there is no photograph of the J'Niah woman.

PART TWO

In which we travel further back in time, before Tanpai, to the island of Quiru, and learn how Dema Ägan became a fugitive, what happened at Korum,
and how she crossed paths with a certain captain...

SEVEN

–From the narrative by Rainer Eicher

Dema found it difficult to sleep. The bed was comfortable, to be sure, and the fireplace, if well-lit and the fire properly tended, made up for the draughty windows. But even so, Dema was a strong woman, a hearty woman of the elements, and neither draught nor rough seas had ever hindered her slumber before.

She lay staring at the ceiling beams of her rented accommodation on Quiru's busy quayside in Sola Din, as she did most nights, her spirit troubled. She had always been focused, in control. Even when she had decided to leave home, all those years ago, there were no endless nights of self-debate, no agonizing over possible outcomes. She simply walked out and away from the violent man she called father, and the useless woman who fell so very short of being a mother.

How, she now wondered, could meeting Meloy and his J'Niah companion change all that, change *her*?

This particular morning, she rose just before dawn, dressed, and slipped out to stroll through Sola Din's silent streets. She hoped the walk would give her clarity.

Her feet now crunched upon the dust and pebbles of a dirt road. Her heart panicked. She had no recollection of leaving the city's boundaries. And when did the sun come up?

Ahead lay the little village of Korum. She felt cold at the notion that she had walked three kilometres and possessed no memory of the journey.

The village was nestled in a small cove. Even through the grey shadows of morning its poverty was obvious—crumbling white plaster exposed red-brick walls beneath; roofing tiles were cracked, and in some places, fragments lay scattered on the ground near foundations; paint flaked from wooden doors.

The tide was out. Beyond the beachhead she saw the wreck of a vessel, a schooner like Meloy's ship, impaled upon the jagged rocks thrusting upward out of the shallows. The victim of a recent storm. The main mast stood bare, its sun-sails missing. The sun-sails on the foremast hung in strips like torn linen, flapping with the help of a mild ocean breeze.

Among the rocks and tidal pools surrounding the wreck a figure moved with great agility, searching the pools between black stones with a restless determination.

Her eyes were rooted upon the figure for several seconds, then she left the road for a narrow trail winding down the grassy hillside. As it deposited her upon the beach she broke into a run, sand pulling at her boots with each stride, until she came to the wreck far out among the rocks.

She did not look at the broken vessel. She stood, breathless, staring at the back of Rymah's head, at the long, glossy black hair that danced across the J'Niah's back.

Rymah cried, "*Sa!*", plunged her hand deep between two black rocks and pulled up a metallic looking object no bigger than her thumb. A piece of machine technology, no doubt washed up by the storm. Rymah turned and held it out to her in one fluid motion.

No shock. No surprise at seeing someone behind her. It was as though, Dema thought, Rymah had expected her to be there.

She looked at Rymah's face, at her smooth, perfect skin, and trembled. It was as though the J'Niah's skin called out to her, an invitation—*touch me! touch me!* Elation—and a dash of fear—welled up inside her.

Rymah now studied the artefact. She wrinkled her forehead, tossed the object away, and went back to searching among the rocks and pools.

Dema tore her gaze away. Her eyes fell upon the wreck, thankful for the distraction it offered.

She caught just enough breath in her throat to say: "I suppose there were no survivors." She moved forward and peered inside the gaping hole in the ship's side.

Not much was left, just bits of wood scattered about, a broken chair and a twisted side table. The electrical box hung on a back wall, its innards spilling out against a blackened panel. It looked as though there had been a small fire. She saw no streaks of acid corrosion coming down from above and figured the battery packs up on deck must still be intact. She was surprised no one had come to remove the packs and dispose of them.

"Looks like she drifted for a long while," she said to herself. "Crew were probably washed overboard before the ship hit ground."

A shadow fell across the hole in the ship. She gasped and spun around. Rymah stood so close Dema could feel her hot breath upon her cheeks. The J'Niah brought her hand up. Sitting in her palm was another artefact, another piece of machine technology, a remnant of a lost people. Like Rymah.

Rymah tapped the top of the object. Tiny needles of bright yellow light shot out from pinpricks scattered over its surface. Dema thought it looked like a star in her hand.

"What is it?" Dema managed to whisper.

A smile lurked at the corner of Rymah's lips. Dema's heart pounded in her ears. Everything about this strange woman, every gesture, every motion of eye or hand, was delicate and precise. Even her proximity, the mere whisper of a touch, was filled with an unknowable energy that set Dema's passions stirring. She had felt it in the *Blue Mariner*. She felt it even more so now.

And it crumbled her resolve, right there, in the shallows, against the shell of the wreck, a sweet magic that took hold and did not let go. Rymah's lips played across Dema's neck and were butterflies brushing against her cheeks. The rhythmic motions of their bodies were not unlike the ocean swells, building and crashing, building and crashing…

And Dema knew—despite the heated madness that sweep through her at that moment—that she would not, could not, wrestle control away from that magic. It would, from this day forward, govern the whole of her existence.

EIGHT

–From the narrative by Rainer Eicher

In the following weeks, Dema had softened her stance toward Captain Meloy. This was no doubt the result of Rymah's influence. One morning, Meloy asked for Dema's help. The repairs to his vessel were completed, but he needed to earn enough to cover the remaining charges. To do that he had to get out onto the sea again.

Dema had used her month's wages to pay the dock master at Sola Din the fee for the use of a rundown schooner called *The Moira*. She possessed old-fashioned canvas sails instead of sun-sails, so battery power would be severely limited.

Dema convinced her own captain, Garbarek, to sign as guarantor for the safe return of the ship. Garbarek was cautious but not overly reluctant. Dema had been sixteen when Garbarek took her on as part of the *Wayfarer*'s crew; they had sailed together for many years now, and the captain had learned to trust her.

The wind had blown steadily for three days. The sails were taut overhead, wind straining them to their limits. At noon on the fourth day she saw the many machines, reaching up like giant, misshapen flowers. As they drew near, she could make out the cables and walkways stretching between them. They reminded her of climbing ivy.

"Take the helm," Meloy said. Dema gripped the wheel as the captain folded the sails away.

Rymah stood in the bow of the ship and was first to

jump over onto the low platform as they came alongside one of the machine stalks.

"Take the pole attachment," Meloy called, and tossed over a long metallic rod. Rymah caught it and in one fluid motion began climbing the stalk to the next platform, some twenty meters up.

Meloy secured the ship to the platform with the mooring lines, tying the vessel up to whatever seemed sturdy: hanging cables, antennae or any other protrusions.

Mooring lines alone would be fine, Dema thought, as long as the sea stayed calm. But the weather shifted quickly out here, and the dark line of cloud to the northeast made her uneasy. If they had to cut and run, they would need a drift-sock to maintain control.

"I don't like the look of those clouds," she said.

Meloy ignored her.

"Shall I ready the drogue? A storm's brewing out there."

"No."

She considered him for a moment. "Captain—"

He looked to the horizon, studied it. She realized he always looked over his shoulder, to the horizon, as though expecting something other than a storm.

"Prepare the nets," he said.

They had gone out on several runs, each time bringing back artefacts to sell in the markets of Sola Din and across the other islands of Quiru. On the last two runs, Meloy did not go with them. He had been offered a temporary job in the dockyard and stayed behind.

Soon Meloy would have enough money to pay for

the release of the *Wave Rider*. Soon he would take Rymah away, off again on the quest. And what then?

The sun lingered in the west, tinting the sky yellow and orange. Dema sat on one of the raised platforms, high above the ship. She swung her legs over the edge and watched the sea sparkle like silver and gold stars. The weather had not turned. The storm she feared had changed direction, run along the horizon, and now raged somewhere in the east.

She looked up to see Rymah standing there. The J'Niah smiled down at her.

"You decide," said Rymah. "Be with us. Yes?"

"I want to." She wrestled with her uncertainty. "But how do I tell my captain? Garbarek has been good to me. She saved my life."

Rymah sank down on her haunches and stroked Dema's arm.

"You be with us," she said. "Is good."

Dema respected her captain, loved her like an older sister. Garbarek was strong and rarely showed emotion. Dema had seen her angry, of course, when a crewmember got something wrong or did not respond fast enough to a command. But that was different. That was part of leadership, of keeping a disciplined crew.

But to join a quest-captain. To travel with a J'Niah, a nomad of the seas. And to what end?

She had seen disappointment in Garbarek's eyes only once and knew it would be painful if that look landed upon her. She did not wish to end her service to Garbarek that way.

And what of Meloy? He welcomed the additional hands on deck, of course. If he resented her closeness with Rymah, felt any bitterness at all, he did not show it.

She reached up and took Rymah's hand in hers. They linked fingers. The warmth of their skin pressed together soothed her conflicted heart.

Rymah stretched out her other hand to the reddening west. "Home," she said, then leaned in and brushed her lips gently over Dema's ears and whispered: *"Together!"*

Dema woke to the sound of a gunshot. She bolted up, steadied herself, and listened. She dismissed the notion of thunder. She had been at sea long enough to distinguish between the two sounds.

Soft morning light bled through the opened hatch above. She squinted into the dimly lit cabin. She was alone.

A second gunshot.

She grabbed her rifle before the sound faded and planted her feet firmly on the floor. She became stone, listening, assessing the situation. She reasoned Rymah was on deck. Although she carried a pistol—at Dema's insistence—the sound Dema heard was loud, thick, booming. Not the high crackling sound a handgun would make.

There! Voices. The thudding of boots above.

With careful steps she moved toward the wooden stairs. She took a few deep breaths, steadied her nerves, and rushed up onto the deck. Rifle firmly in her hands, heart pounding in her ears, she spun around when her feet hit the deck, pointing the gun in all directions.

She was surrounded. There were seven men; some leaned against guide ropes, others stood casually, arms folded across their chests. Their weapons were not drawn, but she knew it made no difference. She would get one shot off before being gunned down.

"Good morning," said a deep voice. "Sorry to wake you so abruptly. Baz was eager to try out his new gun. Can't say I blame him. There's a special thrill in firing a new weapon for the first time. Don't you agree?"

Dema turned. A tall, broad man stepped forward, rifle in hand. Behind him and just slightly to the right she could see Rymah standing in the prow of the ship, alone, head down. On the port side stood a massive, four-sailed vessel. She noticed the tall machines were now in the distance. They must have cut the mooring lines of *The Miora* in the night while she slept.

"Shall I take that?" the man said. He reached forward with his free hand and seized her rifle by the barrel.

Reluctantly, Dema loosened her grip and let him take her weapon. He tossed it overboard.

"You're not the occupant I expected," he said. "But you're not an unpleasant sight."

"Captain Meloy is not here."

"So he isn't," he said. "Pity. I was hoping to catch up with him. We have some business to discuss. No matter. I'll find him." The man looked around. "I heard Meloy had been loaned a new ship, courtesy of a visiting patron. Would that be you, by any chance?"

Dema said nothing.

The man shook his head, waved a hand about. "Bit of an antique, is it?"

"What do you want?"

The man smiled a wide, toothy smile. "I am Captain Ogunwe; my ship is the *Godsong*. To whom do I have the pleasure of addressing?"

She eyed the tall man. Through his smile she sensed a cold and indifferent heart beating behind his broad chest.

Before she could think clearly about her response, her mouth uttered, "I am no one."

"Are you? Ah." He smiled his toothy smile again, then rammed the butt of his rifle into her stomach, sending her crashing to the deck. "Then I guess no one got hurt."

Laughter.

Dema tried to push herself onto her knees.

"Stay down," said Ogunwe.

She did as she was told. While she lay there, she watched some of the men bring up the past day's catch onto the deck. They rifled through the artefacts while the others looked on.

Ogunwe took Rymah's arm and dragged her over to the pile.

"Is it here?" he said.

Rymah kept her head down and remained silent.

Ogunwe stood with his back to Dema. She knew his arms and hands were moving; she knew he was signing to Rymah, but she could not see what he said. But she saw Rymah shake her head at him.

"Did he find it?" said Ogunwe, "Did he hide it somewhere?"

Rymah shook her head again.

"If he did, and you're not telling me—"

They're not interested in just any artefact, Dema realised. They're looking for something specific.

"Take her," he said. A man gripped Rymah's arm. "Check every space on this ship."

"Wait!" Dema got up on one knee. Ogunwe kicked her in the chest, sending her crashing backwards. "Please," she uttered between gasps of air. "*Please!*"

Ogunwe's men ransacked the ship, tossing all the artefacts and any items that were not secured overboard, including everything below deck. Chairs, food, weapons, ammunition, emergency flares, the inflatable life raft, all of it went into the sea.

"There seems to be nothing here," said Ogunwe. He kicked her three more times. "Nothing and no one."

A man came forward, large jugs of oil in each hand. He emptied the contents into the cargo hold. Ogunwe was handed a torch which he tossed into the open hatch of the hold. They crossed back to the *Godsong*.

When she was able to get up the *Godsong* had pulled away and her sun-sails were hoisted, catching the morning wind. Black smoke now billowed from the hold of *The Moira*. Flames roared up. The fire had established itself and was eating away at the old vessel.

She stood there for a moment, stricken with fear. She heard herself call out Rymah's name. Only the wind and the flames answered.

The tall, flower-like machines were not far off. But there were currents between the burning ship and those ancient structures. She just might make it. What other choice did she have?

Without a second thought, she launched herself overboard.

NINE

The account of Otto Sorje, Administrative Officer for the prison at Sola Din, *port of* Quiru.

–From the annals of Avram Aul

…and so Dema Ägan was brought into the quayside's holding cells, kicking and screaming. It was late afternoon. Although her wrists were shackled in front of her and the shackles locked to a chain around her waist, this did not stop the woman from delivering a few mighty blows to one of the two arresting officers. She did this mostly with her head. A constable rushed to help as the battered officer, blood streaming from his nose and mouth, almost beat the woman unconscious.

As they dragged her down the corridor, she kept repeating a woman's name. Rymah, I think she said. (It was all over Sola Din at the time that she was involved with Captain Meloy's J'Niah, so I assume that is the woman in question.)

She was lucky to have been found. A fishing trawler had sent a message and coordinates to every ship in the area that a vessel had been seen on fire near a seafield of machines. A few days later, a cargo ship spotted her on one of the many platforms, waving frantically. (Damned woman was lucky the machines did not discharge, or there would be nothing left of her.) She told them her ship, an old-fashioned schooner she rented from the dock master, Jan Kakhidze, had been attacked by pirates and that this Rymah she kept on about had been forcibly taken.

Whether her story was true or not who can tell? All I know is that when the cargo ship entered the harbour and docked the port authorities were waiting for her. The charge was murder.

Captain Meloy had been due to begin his shift at the dockyard the same morning Dema Ägan sailed off in the old schooner. But he never showed up. It was unusual for him to disappear like that, not from the dockyard at any rate. You see, he spent all his waking hours there; he was working to pay off the repairs to his ship.

Meloy was always about, always visible, a gregarious man and a heavy drinker. That was who he was. I had seen him myself every night at *The Blue Mariner*, telling stories and such. Sometimes he did not go back to his rented room in the village of Korum at all but slept on the benches down by the pier.

Well, a few days later they found him in his rented room, or rather the owner of that establishment in Korum found him. She arrived at around midday and went up to see if he wanted his bedding changed.

There was blood everywhere. It appeared, according to the report, there had been a struggle. It seems Meloy did not go down without a fight. Several blows to the head finally subdued him.

And then he was butchered like an animal.

TEN

–From the narrative by Rainer Eicher

The Officer was a thin man draped in black robes. The robes did not billow and float about his hips and legs when he moved but hung as straight and as heavy as curtains. The impression this gave was that he did not walk but rather floated into her cell, a thin black rod gliding across the stone floor.

"I am the Judicial Officer for this jurisdiction," he said. "But I will not be presiding over your case."

"Oh, no?" Dema said, only half interested in his remarks or his presence.

He shook his head. "Something of this magnitude is not for the Lower Courts. A case like yours is for the Chief Justice of all the islands of Quiru. His court is on our seventh and farthest island. Tomorrow you will be taken there. In five days, he will listen to your case and pass sentence."

Dema turned away and walked to the window. Gripping the iron bars, she stared out toward the harbour, at the various ships coming in and going out. Their tall sun-sails glittering with flecks of sunlight.

"Then why, Mister Judicial Officer of the Lower Courts, are you here?"

"To give you an opportunity," he said, "to change your story."

She rested her head against the iron bars and exhaled. "And why would I do that?"

"If you tell the truth, if you plead guilty, there is a

chance, however small, that you might be spared the death penalty. Make no mistake, you *will* be found guilty of murder. We both know this."

"I've told you what happened."

"Give yourself a fighting chance," he said. "Believe it or not, I do not wish to see you put to death."

She scoffed. "How noble of you." She banged her head twice against the bars. "My story stands. The facts are the facts, and I cannot—"

"The facts are as follows, as established by eyewitness accounts: you spent most if not all of your free time with Captain Meloy, had an affair with his J'Niah companion. You became obsessed with her. He would not give her over to you, nor would he take you on as a permanent member of his crew. You argued that fateful morning, and in a fit of blind jealousy you killed him, took the J'Niah, and fled. The fire must have been accidental and so you lost the ship and your means of escape."

"That's *your* story."

"It can be yours, if you cooperate." He came up behind her and spoke over her shoulder. "Blind jealousy can be synonymous with temporary insanity. That is the key. Plead guilty on those grounds and you might be spared."

"But that's not the way it happened!"

"The witnesses cannot be disputed. You were seen by dozens of people with the J'Niah, with Captain Meloy. In *The Blue Mariner* you were heard to ridicule him, argue with him on more than one occasion. You were seen many times in Korum, and you were seen leaving his room on the last day he was known to be alive."

"In some countries I've visited those accounts would make me a suspect," she said. "But it would take more than that for a conviction."

He narrowed his eyes. "Some countries aren't as quick to administer justice as we are."

"Flimsy eyewitness accounts and hearsay. So that's Quiru justice, is it?"

"You've spent time in our jails before," he said. "For causing disturbances, violence. Were the eyewitnesses wrong about your crimes? Did you not commit such acts?"

She kept her back to him and said nothing.

"Others have known the madness that comes with being with a J'Niah," he said. "Many shun them for this reason." He placed a hand upon her shoulder. "Madness." He shook her gently. "That is all it is."

She brushed his hand away and moved to the far wall. To her it did not feel like madness, was not madness. How could it be? She felt sick to her stomach. They wanted her to be guilty, and she knew they would find her guilty. Though she knew the chances of being spared death were remote, the idea of lying to possibly save her own life felt like a betrayal of Rymah's memory.

"Where is the J'Niah?" he asked.

"I don't know. I told you, they took her."

"This Captain Ogunwe you spoke of? I'm sorry, but no other vessel was seen in the area around the time of your ill-fated voyage out to the machines. No. We can assume this Rymah person escaped in *Moira's* lifepod."

"That ship carried no lifepod."

"I see. Well, without any witnesses, no additional charges can be brought against you. I will list the

J'Niah's whereabouts as unknown."

She wondered if Rymah truly was dead.

Most likely, she concluded, and the thought nearly crushed her.

"Now, focus for me," the man prodded, "and let's start again…"

"Leave now," she said.

He sighed heavily.

"As you wish," he said. "But think carefully how you might proceed, and remember, you can expect no help from Garbarek. You have brought shame upon your captain and brought into question her judgement of character. Because of this, Garbarek and the rest of her crew have abandoned you. The *Wayfarer* has sailed, leaving you alone to face the charge of murder."

The door closed and locked. His footsteps faded down the corridor. She stood in the silence, unmoving, for some time.

When night fell upon the room and the light drained away, she collapsed to the floor and sobbed.

ELEVEN

Fragmented accounts of Dema Ägan's early years, compiled here in one narrative (authors unknown).

–From the annals of Avram Aul

At thirteen years of age she began using the name Dema Ägan and took to the sea. It was not an easy decision. But it really was the only one available. Of the few who survived the outbreak that hit the Far Northern Isles, not many chose to stay on.

Just over five thousand people lived across those four Isles. By the time the disease ran its course roughly six hundred remained. The port city of Gard—the only major city among the Isles—was deserted, an empty husk, and stayed that way for years after. Small towns and villages were either dead or reduced to enclaves of desperate survivors.

Few ships travelled that far north. Of those that did many refused to land there, even after the quarantine had been lifted.

The surviving children were shared out among the remaining adult population. Before she changed her name Dema, along with three siblings, were placed with a middle-aged couple and an old man on a small farm. (It is not known whether these siblings were Dema's actual blood relatives or not. Records of that tumultuous time were destroyed by fire, as authorities set about burning homes, municipal buildings or whole villages in an attempt to purge the disease. Any remaining records lay incomplete.)

The locals said that the man of the farm was a brute and a drunk, and the woman did nothing more than endure him. The old man Dema and the other children called "grandfather" cared for them as best he could. When the old man died, the limited protection he offered the children died with him.

The children worked hard. The small holding was far up the side of a rocky hill. It was far enough away from the town that the only residents who could hear the screams from the nightly beatings were the goats that bleated outside on the harsh grass.

On her thirteenth birthday, Dema broke into a locked cupboard in the farmhouse, stole some money, and left under cover of darkness. She fled her island home and worked her way across the sea in a south by southeast direction, taking up any menial work she could get with any captain who would take someone so young; scrubbing decks, working in the galley, or loading and unloading cargo.

When a particular job no longer suited her, or when she became dissatisfied with the ship or crew she worked with, she would depart at the next stop. On the Islands of Gish, Dema waited many weeks for another opportunity. The departure manifest hung on the outside wall of the harbour inn. She checked it every day and offered her labour to many disinterested ship captains.

One captain, who no doubt wanted to get rid of the girl, told her that if she wanted work she needed to get to the Confederate Archipelago. There were three massive ports there, and lots of work to be had. Unfortunately, he could not take her. He was heading in the wrong direction. But he knew of someone who could and pointed to the massive ship that had come in for repairs that morning.

At the ship's gangplank stood the captain, a tall woman, thin and lean. Her name was Tove Garbarek. She looked annoyed when Dema shoved all the money she had into her hand.

"You need to pay at the office," Garbarek said, "write your name on the manifest and get a receipt. They take their cut, and I get the rest. That's how it works."

Dema stood there, silently, staring into her weather-worn face.

"A dockhand will come aboard and check receipt numbers against the ones on the office passenger list," Garbarek said. "They won't let us cast off otherwise. You have to do it proper."

Dema remained rooted in place.

Garbarek frowned. "You're a bit young, aren't you? Someone will want to know where you're going and where to find you."

Dema shook her head with great vigour.

Garbarek looked at her face—really looked at her. Dema quickly pulled her hair across her forehead but Garbarek swatted her hand away and lifted the hair above the girl's forehead. There was a bruise just at her hairline. Then she reached out and yanked Dema's coat off one shoulder. Dema wore a shirt with the sleeves cut off and so her upper arm was exposed. She could see the purple marks there, like tattoos. Garbarek's face grew dark.

Dema hesitated, then said, "My…thighs are much the same, Mistress."

Garbarek pulled Dema's coat back up and gently covered the girl's arm. "What mariner did this? What ship? I want names."

"That mariner is far behind me," Dema said, "as is the man I once called father."

In that moment, Garbarek understood. She adjusted her own long coat and took a quick glance about. She shoved the money into Dema's coat pocket.

"I need another rigger," she said. "Are you up for it?"

"Yes, Mistress Captain."

Garbarek nodded. "I'll sign you on as part of my crew. Be warned, I run a strict ship. Work hard and in everything you do, be precise."

"Yes, Mistress Captain."

She pointed a finger in Dema's face but there was no malice in her actions or her voice. "I trust you won't make me regret this."

TWELVE

–From the narrative by Rainer Eicher

The land ahead lay desolate. The beachhead of the farthest island of Quiru was nothing more than a pile of crumbling grey stone. The air here was motionless, and even the light seemed diffused, muted, as though some unseen filter stretched over the island.

It made Dema feel trapped, hopeless. *But then*, she thought, wrists bruised and pulsing within their iron shackles, *that is the purpose of this place*.

The two men with her, Ghent and Rebus, mumbled to each other as they rowed the skiff to shore.

She looked back across the water, at the ship now sailing away, and felt a stirring within her: a stirring for winds and currents and far places, and the prospect of freedom they offered. Freedom for both her and Rymah.

But why accommodate that desire any longer? As quickly as Rymah had entered her life, she was now gone. And where would Dema want to go without her? The winds and currents that had been a large part of her life now offered her nothing but vast lonely spaces.

Madness, the Judicial Officer of the Lower Courts had called it.

Maybe so, she thought. After all, Dema would have gone anywhere with her, even to the ends of the uncharted world where they would, most likely, meet their destruction.

But at least they would have died together.

Now she faced the prospect of dying alone.

Ghent and Rebus stowed their oars and leapt into the water. Grunting, they pulled the boat up onto the barren shore. When it was secured Ghent helped Dema out, gripped her chain, and led her onto the grey land.

Far up from the shoreline was a large iron brazier resting on a flat-topped boulder which jutted out of the ground. Rebus pulled a canister out of a small chest in the back of the boat. He walked to the boulder, climbed up the crude steps carved into its side, and poured the contents of the canister onto the wood in the brazier. He lit a match and tossed it in. Flames exploded into the sky.

A signal they had arrived.

Primitive, she thought, but understandable. She had seen no outward signs of technology. And deforestation and scrub fires, she had learned, had cleansed away the flesh of Quiru's farthest island, down to its rocky bones.

No way for a prisoner to communicate with anyone on or off the island.

No places to hide.

Upon a distant hill a red fire now burned in response. The message of their arrival would be communicated this way, from hill to hill, until it reached the eyes of those who guarded the penitentiary walls.

The court-and-prison complex was a single, great stone fortress, and it lay at the heart of the grey island, a four-day journey inland. The Chief Justice, she knew, was there, waiting for her.

"Come!" Ghent pulled her chain and began walking up the shore. Rebus followed.

They came to a cobbled road. A brick bungalow sat off to the right. As they approached, she smelled horses and heard the occasional stomping of hooves coming from the yard behind the building.

A bald man walked out of the small house, armed with a rifle, and greeted her captors. They spoke in low voices. When it seemed they had agreed upon something, the bald man put his fingers in his mouth and whistled. Two black horses came around the side of the bungalow, pulling a black carriage. Another man, much older, was seated up in the driver's box.

"Lock her in," said the driver. "I'd like to get to the first station while we still have the day."

Dema was locked in the coach. She looked through the barred windows. Two more horses were brought out, sheathed rifles and extra ammunition strapped to the side of the saddles. Ghent and Rebus climbed into the saddles, and each took a position on either side of the carriage.

They struck out on the cobbled road, slow and deliberate, as though pulling a hearse, a silent dirge playing across the dead, grey land.

Night covered everything when they reached the first station. Although the moon should be rising, clouds blanketed the island in darkness. The flames from the torches the men now held created small globes of red light around them.

She heard Ghent and Rebus dismount. They placed the torches in iron mounts stuck into the ground. The driver came down from his seat, dug in his pocket, and produced a set of keys. He unlocked the carriage door. "Out!"

When she did not move fast enough, he reached in,

grabbed her arm, pulled her out, and threw her to the ground. Ghent and Rebus laughed.

"Get her inside," said the driver. "I'll unload the dry food from the carriage. One of you stable the horses out back."

"I got it," said Rebus.

The driver turned to Ghent. "There are two beds inside. You two can take them. When the weather's warm and dry, I like to sleep outside. No, those aren't rain clouds."

Ghent snorted. "I know what a rain cloud looks like."

"Wasn't so sure," said the driver. "You looked wet behind the ears to me."

"Don't get smart, old man," said Ghent. "I did my time in the navy." Then he dragged Dema up onto her feet, led her up the steps, across the wooden planks of the porch, and into the station. It was cold inside and smelled of stone and dust. A match was struck, and an oil lamp bathed the room in a soft yellow light. There was a table and chairs at one end of the room, two beds at the other end.

"Over here." Ghent pushed her toward another room near the back. He shoved her in, closed the thick, wooden door and locked it.

It was pitch black inside. There was no window. Feeling around in the dark she discovered there was neither table nor bed: just stone walls and a stone floor. She squatted down in a corner and drew her legs up and rested her head upon her knees. The chill in the room bit through her clothes and made her shiver.

But the cold made little difference to her. She was tired, and no longer wished to wrestle with her thoughts. Sleep was like a dark pool rising around her; it rose until it covered her, and she let herself be drowned in it.

When she woke, she found herself bathed in rays of warm yellow light flooding in from the other room beyond the opened door.

"Morning already?" she moaned into her sleeve.

"On your feet and out!"

Dema's ears pricked, and in those first few seconds she was overcome with confusion.

A darkened figure ran into the room, keys jangling. The figure unlocked her shackles and threw them aside. They disappeared into a shaded corner and clanked against unseen stone.

"I said get out, Boatswain!"

"Mistress Captain?"

"Let's go." Garbarek pulled her up to her feet and led her out into the yellow light. Dema's captors, Ghent and Rebus, lay in their beds, throats slit from ear to ear.

Outside, the clouds had gone, and the moon was out and high in the sky, full and bold. She could see the driver's body lying prostrate on the porch in the moonlight. A dark pool was spread out around his head, staining the wooden planks.

Dema took a few seconds to process all that she had just seen, the bodies, the blood. She had seen bloodshed many times, had seen her captain cut down men and woman with ease, pirates mostly. So why did it shock her now?

Because these were men of the authorities.

As if she could read Dema's mind, Garbarek said,

"Didn't think I had it in me, did you? Now you know something new about me. And I'll survive this. The only witness is you. I doubt you'll suddenly turn me in. And by the way, you're welcome."

Garbarek had a reputation for being head-strong, honest, noble, and could talk herself around to any point of view, if the need demanded it.

"Mistress Captain, how—"

"Finding you wasn't difficult. It was no secret where they were taking you. Those fools made it easy with their blasted torches. Just because no one has ever attempted a jail break on this island before doesn't mean you shouldn't be prepared for one."

"I was told you sailed," Dema said and stumbled down the steps.

"We did," said Garbarek. Something unspoken lay in the lines of her face, the almond curves of her eyes. "Believe me, I had to convince myself to come back for you."

Dema heard something different in her captain's voice, something she had heard only once before. Disappointment, for sure. Possibly heartbreak.

Garbarek went silent, composed herself. Dema knew her captain was thinking of what her next words might be.

"You are an exceptional mariner," Garbarek said. "But your quick temper has been a blight upon me and my ship for too long. Frankly, I am surprised this did not happen sooner."

"But you believe me. That I didn't kill Captain Meloy."

"Your innocence was never in question," said

Garbarek. "Although your judgment leaves a lot to be desired."

She could not look Garbarek in the eyes.

"It had come to my attention that your friend, Captain Meloy," said Garbarek, "had some rather disreputable connections. I told the authorities of my concerns and protested your innocence. Meloy either knew something and was killed for it, provided something and served his purpose, or failed to deliver. Of course, I cannot prove any of this—no witnesses—and the authorities dismissed it as wild speculation. So, I paid for your mistake and left."

"I'm sorry about *The Moira*."

"Dema, listen," said Garbarek. "The *Wayfarer* is anchored at an atoll not far from here. I left the First Officer in charge. Told him I was taking the skiff around to the other side of the atoll. I must get back before he thinks I have been gone too long. The skiff is beached up the coast, in that direction." She pointed northwest.

"And the crew? Do they know?"

Garbarek shook her head. "I sent the crew ashore. Further leave. There is a small community on that atoll. Independent. Free-spirited. The crew can enjoy themselves once more before we quit this part of the world. Not one could say they had any knowledge of this."

Cold fingers ran up Dema's body. She knew the answer to her next question, but she asked it all the same: "I will not be coming with you, will I?"

"No. As far as the crew are concerned you have shamed us all, and they have excised you from their minds and hearts."

"I understand, Mistress." Her own heart felt heavy

with a burning sorrow. It was the same feeling she had when she fled her island home, knowing she was leaving the other children behind. Knowing she would never see them again.

But this time, it was she who was being left behind.

"I thank you for taking me on as one of your crew," Dema said, "for your kindness to me."

Garbarek did something Dema had never seen her captain do before: she hesitated. There was something Garbarek wanted to say, her eyes betrayed a hint of emotion and her lips moved ever so slightly.

Then she stiffened, taking on her usual air of authority, and her face became stone in the moonlight. Whatever Garbarek had wanted to say, whatever was on her heart, was gone.

"I am here because I owe you, Dema. I was fortunate you were there when we fought off the Ahani raiders. You saved my life then; tonight, we are even."

"And now?"

"You will head due west," said Garbarek. "There is a cove there. After paying for *The Moira*, I used my remaining reserves to purchase a small ship through a third party. I've enlisted the services of a mariner I know who, shall we say, wishes to avoid contact with authorities of any kind. He is an expert navigator and will take you far away from here. Now go around back and get us some horses."

Dema did as she was told. When she returned, Garbarek threw her a pistol.

"If it comes to it," Garbarek said, "if something happens, and they somehow catch up with you, better to do it yourself."

Dema considered her captain's words, then tucked the weapon under her belt.

"We have five hours of night left," said Garbarek, "and this road has not yet turned in toward the heart of this island, which means we are a little over four hours from the western coast. If you keep going, you can reach the cove before the dawn breaks."

Dema mounted and grabbed the reins.

"Remember, the ship is small, more like a schooner," Garbarek said, "and as such does not carry a skiff, just a lifepod. It will anchor as close to shore as possible, so you'll have to swim out to it."

Dema frowned. "Not the first time I have had to swim to safety."

Garbarek mounted the other horse. "Dema, understand this: wherever you go, never breathe my name out of your mouth. No one must know what I did here this night. For you."

"As always, Mistress Captain, you have my solemn word."

Garbarek hesitated again, as if wanting to say something more. Her shoulders slumped forward, and it looked as though Garbarek might throw herself forward and embrace her. Instead, she danced her horse a few paces away, opening up a chasm between them.

Dema bowed. "Mistress Captain."

"Farewell, Boatswain. We will never see each other again. Ever." Garbarek jerked the reins, turned her horse northwest, and rode off.

Dema, overrun with grief, watched her captain go, a pale spectre fading into the night beyond the cold moonlight.

THIRTEEN

–From the narrative by Rainer Eicher

Panting and tossing its head about, Dema's horse had stopped and would go no further. There were no pools of fresh water for the animal to drink from, nothing to eat. She knew that unless someone found the beast it would certainly die. There was nothing she could do. She thanked the animal for its service, kissed its head, and struck out on foot, running as fast as her feet would allow.

Dawn was struggling to break when she reached the western coast. The moon should be sitting low in front of her, but it was not there. The clouds had returned to claim the sky. Behind her in the east, a thin line of muted grey light appeared on the horizon. The air was damp and heavy with salt.

She had been travelling for a little over an hour, she reckoned, and she was tired. The rough leather of her boots rubbed her ankles raw. She could feel the blood, warm and wet, pooling at her heels.

Standing now at the top of a granite cliff, she looked down at the shadowy cove spread out beneath her. Her brow creased with frustration. The sea was gone. A fog had rolled in and was now making a slow dance up across the beachhead.

She squinted hard into the murky greyness, hoping to catch the angular shadows of a ship, the tall line of a mast.

Nothing.

But the ship was out there. Somewhere. Garbarek was always as good as her word.

She thought she heard a faint sound, off in the distance. She cocked her head and listened. It was gone.

She walked to where the cliff sloped downward. It would be easier to climb down from there, for there were many rocks and boulders upon which she could descend. When she reached the bottom, her vision was reduced to within an arm's length.

She took a step forward. The crunch beneath her feet told her it was a pebbled beach. The gentle splash of the surf told her ears the sea was off to her left, and she walked until the water splattered under her boots. She paced up and down the waterline, peering into the gloom.

The ship is small, like a schooner. You will have to swim out to it.

"Yes," she heard herself say, "but in which direction?"

Then she heard it again. That sound. This time it was closer and she recognized it. A bell.

One strike—then silence.

She pulled off her boots, tossed them aside, and waded into the sea until it was up to her waist. She ignored the sting of salt-water at her ankles. Despite the fog, she knew the morning was fast approaching; a muddied light was seeping into the sky.

She walked into the sea, until the water covered her shoulders. And she waited.

"Come on..."

It would be late in the new day before anyone suspected something was wrong and sent out a patrol.

"Come on..."

But having half a day's grace did not calm her nerves. She needed to leave now, to put as much distance between her and this island as possible. To make the most of this opportunity her captain had given her. It would not come again.

"Come on…"

Another strike.

There! She judged the direction the sound was coming from and began to swim. When she felt she had swum far enough she stopped and looked around. The fog was thicker out here, and she could see no ship.

Panic set in.

"Hello," she called out. "Hello to the ship!"

She turned around in circles several times and only now noticed how cold the water was.

"Hello to the ship!"

The ring of a bell, high and clear and off to her left. She began to swim toward it when a giant shadow burst through the fog and came up alongside her. She recoiled, kicking back with her legs, pushing herself away before she slammed into the ship's hull.

"Hello, to the swimmer!" A man's voice. She reasoned he was the navigator Garbarek told her of. Dema noticed the purr of an electric motor, and the sails were furled.

She swam up to the side of the ship. A hand reached down out of the mist. Dema stretched her own hand up toward it and took hold of the arm below the elbow. The other person gripped Dema's arm in the same fashion and began to pull. She heaved herself up the side of the ship and threw her other arm over the railing to gain a purchase. She took a deep breath, gathered her strength, and pulled herself up to stare into a familiar face.

"Rymah!"

The J'Niah smiled down at her, then leaned forward and kissed her. Before Dema could find any words to speak, Rymah helped her onto the deck.

"How?" Dema took Rymah's head into her hands, let her eyes roam over every inch of the other woman's face. "I saw them take you...I thought you were dead...I thought..."

"I escape." Rymah smiled again. "I have ways."

Of that Dema was sure. She threw her arms around the woman and hugged her fiercely. A thousand words competed for her tongue, but all she could do was hold Rymah close.

"I heard you survived," Rymah said. "One of Ogunwe's men, he went ashore. Heard you were blamed for Meloy's death. Ogunwe wanted his ship. 'Compensation', he called it, for wasting his time."

"If you please, ladies." The navigator stood by the wheel.

Dema let Rymah go and did her best to swallow her heart. "Permission to come aboard."

"No formalities required," he said. "And you don't need permission to board your own vessel, Mistress Captain. But we do need to go."

She was struck by confusion. *My vessel...* She surveyed the ship.

"This is the *Wave Rider*!"

"Yes, Mistress Captain," said the navigator.

When one of Ogunwe's men went to take charge of it, Rymah signed, *it was gone.*

"Of course it was," Dema said. "So, this is the ship

Garbarek purchased."

No one came forward, Rymah signed, *to pay the remaining charges. The ship took up space. Harbour master needed to get rid of it.*

"Mistress Captain, we can't sit here. The fog won't last forever."

"But, Rymah, how did you know Garbarek was coming for me?"

"She's a J'Niah," the navigator said, as if that was an answer in itself.

And when Dema thought about it, she knew it was.

"So you took her aboard," she said to the Navigator.

"I'd be a fool not to," he replied. "we're in a desperate situation, you and me. When a J'Niah sorceress comes and offers help, you take it." He turned to Rymah. "Whatever it is you're going to do, better do it now."

Rymah took her hand and led her to the wheel. Dema had noticed the item fixed below the wheel before and had thought it merely decorative.

Then she remembered one part of her conversation with Meloy.

...I've seen your ship!...

...No, you haven't. Not really...

"So that's what he meant." She looked at the artefact, then to Rymah. "Machine technology. Was this how he travelled?"

Rymah smiled, then placed Dema's hand over the device and ran her fingers along the side of it. There was a flash of blue light, followed by the sting of searing heat. She wanted to pull her hand away but Rymah held it there.

The heat dissipated, and Dema's hand now felt ice-cold. Rymah let her go. Dema took her hand away and examined it. There were no burns. The skin was healthy.

"We go," said Rymah. "Far away. You are now the key."

Dema, staring at her palm, understood.

"Navigator," she said. "Let's raise the sun-sails."

"Aye, Mistress Captain."

When they had gotten the sails up, he returned to the wheel and turned the ship about. He put the electric engine in neutral. The morning's breeze took hold of the sails and the ship began to move.

"Recommendations for heading, Navigator," she said.

"South-by-southeast. There's a wide expanse there. We can disappear for a little while and discuss our future."

"Set your course, south-by-southeast."

"Aye, Mistress Captain." When he had set the ship's course, he stepped aside for her to touch the device.

"We go," Rymah said.

"Far away," Dema replied, and she palmed the device under the wheel. There was a flash, a feeling of movement, and the fog was gone.

The *Wave Rider* now sailed under a clear sky. The sun was a yellow-orange ball on the eastern horizon, and all around them the sea was empty. No ships. No land. Nothing but the wind in her ears and the currents beneath her ship.

She was free.

"Thank you, my captain," Dema whispered to the air, "and goodbye."

a loose pane of glass

The dark of night has brought with it a penetrating wind. In a partially opened window, a loose pane of glass shudders in rhythm with my racing heart.

It is all there in Rainer Eicher's book, printed across the pages in my hands: the frustration, the hopelessness of sitting in that cell; the exultation at her reunion with Rymah; the weight of despair at having to leave behind her captain and crew.

And what makes my heart beat with such force is that I can see her, swimming for her life, sailing south-by-southeast in the *Wave Rider*, speeding toward salvation, her J'Niah lover by her side...

As if sensing the many thoughts swimming in my head, the Director appears.

"Troubled?" he says, with a tone that suggests he expects me to be.

"Garbarek should have left Dema behind." I hear my voice: it sounds muted, grainy, as if my throat is stuffed with sand.

"Tove Garbarek was everything a righteous ship's captain should be," he says. "Even today, her stories are looked upon with great favour."

"Which is why I cannot believe she would risk her reputation—"

"Garbarek's stories are told to children and apprentices, as a model to emulate. A hero of discipline, authority. And in that regard, the stories do her justice."

He shakes his head. "But sometimes even a ship's captain must be more than that, or the story is incomplete."

"Discipline is crucial to survival, and reputation is the key to trust."

He sighs. "You speak those words as though they were a mantra, like a school-child would."

Though I detect no malice in his words, they sting, nonetheless.

"You may question Tove Garbarek's judgement," he says, "but trust is built on more than reputation alone."

Somehow, I know he is right, but my bitterness refuses to allow me to accept his words.

"You think I do not understand who Dema is," I say, "the things she has done? You show me a book no one has ever seen, a story no one has heard, and this changes what?"

The Director clasps his hands together, and for the briefest of seconds he seems hesitant, as though there is something perched on the edge of his tongue.

"Am I supposed to now feel sympathy for her? Is that what you want, Director?"

He searches my face, then purses his lips and sighs through his nose. "Finish the story," he says, softly. "Then maybe things will be clear for you."

He leaves as quietly as he came.

I feel as though the air has been sucked out of the room with his departure. My chest burns for want of more air. My head swims and my vision darkens all around, until I can only see the brown stone of the window ledge before me.

Clear? What does he want to be clear? Dema Ägan, the victim, the innocent one fate had conspired against?

Once, the very idea would have churned my stomach. But now...

I look down at the book. I have crumpled the page in my hand.

PART THREE

In which we now return to the waters near Tanpai,
learn of Kerrod's dark pursuit,
the power of Rymah's need, and
the cost of Dema's secret voyage…

FOURTEEN

–From the narrative by Rainer Eicher

Out here, due south of Tanpai, the ocean seemed to go on and on, a turquoise sheet stretching toward eternity. It was as if, Dema thought, they were the only people alive on an endless ocean world.

With the displacement device, a voyage of seven weeks lasted barely two. But it was two weeks of Dema looking over her shoulder at Kerrod and his men, Tevis and Kilso; two weeks of being separated from Rymah by the deck beneath her feet; two weeks of agonizing uncertainty. Kerrod refused to let them speak to each other, refused to let them be near each other, and Dema spent most nights topside.

They spent their time meeting vessels outside normal trade lanes, exchanging cargo: armaments, machine artefacts of note. On two occasions another vessel hung in the distance for several minutes, as though trailing them, before slipping below the horizon.

On the fifteenth day they entered a sea-field of machines, basking in the orange glow of a late afternoon sun. Waiting.

Kerrod came and stood beside her. He looked up at the sea-stalks, which towered over them like threatening sentinels.

"Worried?" Dema asked. "I'm sure Rymah told you these stalks won't discharge for some time."

"She did," he said. "Remarkable how she can know such things."

Dema shrugged. "She simply knows. When you see her panic, we'll have but a few minutes to put good distance between ourselves and those machines."

He acknowledged her words with a small nod.

"And you're still worried." Dema sneered. "Now is not the time to realise you can't stomach a little uncertainty."

He looked through her, as though she were not there. It made her feel cold inside, but she refused to show her fear. Her grin widened until it raised her cheeks up under her eyes.

"This is the spot," he said. "Hold us here." He motioned to Kilso. "A ship will come somewhere along this route. Raise the first signal flag."

"Aye, sir," the man said, and moved toward the main sail.

Kerrod walked to the bow.

A voice said: "Why do you antagonize him?"

She turned to the youth sitting on the deck to her left. He was Selasi, the boy from the dock at Tanpai. Both legs were folded in front of him. He brought one leg up, rested his arm on his knee, and twirled a pen between his thin fingers. The other hand held the leather-bound book in which he was writing. He pressed it close against his bare chest.

She smiled wickedly. "Because I don't ever want that steaming pile of shit to think he has me," she said, then leaned over. "And you can write that down in your book, boy."

And he did something that surprised her: he laughed. A beautiful, childish laugh.

"I think I will." He stood up, then as if struck by an

unseen hand, the spirit of gaiety fled from his face.

"What troubles you, boy?"

He swallowed. "What happened in Tanpai, that evening, how you were captured…I am truly sorry, Mistress, that I took part in such a thing, and I—"

"You keep trying to bring this matter up. It bothers you, doesn't it?"

"Yes, Mistress."

"And I'll tell you again, Selasi, put your mind at rest," she said. "Knowing Kerrod, you probably had little choice in the matter."

Relief flushed his cheeks, and he thanked her. He then spotted Rymah near the bow.

"The J'Niah, Rymah…"

She kept her hands on the wheel, gripped it so her knuckles turned white.

"What of her?"

"He secures you for this job, and she's the guarantor," he said. Not a question but a statement. "An unusual arrangement to be sure but one that, I assume, secures your loyalty."

"Loyalty." She spat. "The bastard doesn't know what the word means." She gazed at the back of Rymah's head. The prospect of yet another failure weighed Dema down. She had risked both their lives on more than one occasion. But not like this. Never before had their survival been placed so securely in the hands of another. And Kerrod was a powerful man, powerful enough to take leave of his position during the season's busiest time for Tanpai.

"You see much, young Selasi," she said.

"A good bard is a keen observer, Mistress Captain."

She frowned. "Then you well know, Selasi the Good Bard, that if one is cautious, vigilant—a keen observer, as you say—an opportunity will present itself." She raised her eyebrows. "If you catch my meaning."

He nodded. "And that's the story every ship's bard hopes to write," he said. "Our hero, weighed down by grief, backed into a corner, yet strong and ever watchful, waiting for her chance…"

"He hires *you* as his bard, to record his exploits for posterity and whatever dark gods he worships, yet you think me the hero, huh?"

Selasi blushed.

She wanted to smile, thank him for his adoration but she became sombre instead. She thought of her island home in the far north, of the farm on the hillside, and the children she had once tried to protect. Children she had abandoned. Left behind.

When she thought about it now, she could find no good reason why she did it. None that would exonerate her from the guilt that haunted her. She had given in to her fear, succumbed to the instinct to survive above all else. It was, she believed, the most unforgiveable of all sins.

A deep and profound sadness grew around her eyes.

She placed her hand on the boy's head.

"Don't observe that idea too deeply, young Selasi," she said. "You may not like what you find."

Evening was fast approaching when Tevis came bounding up from the stern. "Kerrod!" He pointed to the perimeter of the sea-field. A Karahsek vessel sailed silently between the ancient sea-stalks.

"They're not responding," said Kilso.

"Raise the second flag," Kerrod said.

The vessel ignored them.

Kerrod exhaled. "Raise the third flag! They have to answer the call of a Regent messenger."

For a moment the ship kept its course, then changed direction and headed toward them.

"Keep your guns hidden but within easy reach," Kerrod said.

"Not the trusting type, are you?" Dema muttered.

Kerrod ignored her. "And get the J'Niah below deck, Tevis. Can't risk losing her."

Rymah tried to sign but Kerrod stopped her with a gesture.

"I didn't know you spoke J'Niah," Dema said. He continued to ignore her.

Tevis returned from locking Rymah below while Kilso took to the *Sceptre*'s bow, eyes searching the length of the Karahsek vessel.

The other ship, larger than the *Sceptre* and with a six-man crew on deck, progressed slowly through the seafield until they were side-by-side.

Dema jumped at the sudden sound of an explosion. Selasi threw himself to the deck, book clasped firmly in his arms.

Wooden shrapnel pelted the *Sceptre*, the machine-stalks. Kilso, grenade-launcher resting on his shoulder, had blasted out the other ship's engine shaft. Black smoke rose up from the Karahsek vessel like a blooming flower. A small fire took hold.

The Karahsek mariners panicked, shouted.

Selasi raised his head.

"Stay down, boy!" Dema said.

"What's he doing?"

"Just stay where you are."

The sounds of chaos filled the air.

"On your knees!" Kerrod shouted, jumping onboard the Karahsek ship, pistols in both hands. "Hands above you!" Two men tried to reach for their weapons, but Kerrod gunned them down.

Tevis secured the two ships with hooks, and then followed him aboard the Karahsek vessel and went below deck.

Dema glanced at the lifepod, secured to the rear back quarter of her ship. She knew she had only a matter of seconds to take advantage of the turmoil…

But Rymah was locked below.

She looked to the boy. She mouthed the word "Go!" and nodded to the pod. The boy glanced at it and shook his head.

"Don't be a fool," she said between teeth. "I don't know what he's doing. I don't know what his goal is, but he may get us all killed."

Selasi looked over at the other ship. "I think he has the advantage, this time."

"*Selasi—*"

"I stay with you, Mistress Captain."

She was about to say something when she saw Tevis return from below. He walked across the deck of the Karahsek ship, a fat satchel in one hand and dragging a J'Niah woman with the other.

Tevis held the bag up. "I think this is it."

Kerrod spoke to the J'Niah, "Is that the artefact?"

She said that it was.

With a nod from Kerrod, Tevis tossed the heavy bag aboard the *Sceptre*. Kilso caught it.

"Betrayer!" one of the Karahsek men growled. "When the Dictate hears of this—"

Kerrod shot him in the head.

"And her?" asked Tevis. "Do we take her?"

"No," Kerrod replied. "Ever seen two J'Niahs in the same place? They'll tear each other apart like bull dogs in the same kennel."

Tevis drew forth a knife from under his tunic, slit the woman's throat, and pushed her overboard.

They jumped back aboard the *Sceptre*, and Kilso unhooked the ships. Dema drew up full sails which caught the wind and sun. Behind them, the burning Karahsek ship drifted deeper into the sea-field of machines.

Kerrod ordered Tevis below. Dema realised it was to watch Rymah. Moments later he popped his head through the hole. "She's having a fit, Kerrod!"

Dema palmed the device. The air around them appeared to ripple. The ancient sea-machines were now far behind on the horizon.

Despite the distance the whine and drone of the machines filled the air. The darkening sky cracked open. A dozen blinding lights shot upward from the stalks and pierced the sky above, slitting it open as though it were nothing more than a tarpaulin stretched above them.

Though Dema knew it was impossible, she swore she could hear the screaming of the Karahsek men as the searing heat cooked them alive.

FIFTEEN

An eyewitness interviewed, compiled and edited for this edition.

–From the annals of Avram Aul

State your name and occupation for the record, please.

My name is Saga Pihl. I am ship's bard for the *Red Sky*, a trading vessel from the Island of Friis.

Ship's compliment was fourteen that day.

I did not ask you for the ship's compliment. Please answer only the questions put to you. Now, where did your ship stop and what happened after that?

We were three days out from the substation on equatorial Tava. We'd stopped there to replenish our water supply and take on some crates of potatoes and dried fish so we could complete our journey. Our destination was the Islands of Moa in the South Seas.

They came out of nowhere. One minute the sea was empty all around us; suddenly a ship appeared, as if out of thin air.

Name the ship for the record, please.

She was the *Sceptre of Night*, commanded by Dema Ägan. They took us by surprise, managed to gun down three of our crew before a soul could raise a weapon. Being more agile than the *Red Sky*, she was alongside us before we could regroup and return fire. Then they boarded us. Eight of them. Five were wild men from the Iron Fortress, the floating city. Rumour had it the *Sceptre* often visited that sinister place, and sometimes took its men as additional crew.

And Dema Ägan? Did she board the *Red Sky*?

No. She stayed on her ship and simply watched, cold, unmoving. It chilled me to see her just stand there, as two of the wild men bludgeoned our captain to death. We tried to fight back, but they had the advantage. Killed another three of us. We surrendered immediately.

What did they want?

A passenger. They said they would let us go if we handed him over. But I knew they weren't going to let us sail away.

Can you tell us anything about this passenger?

No. Anonymity was his concern, and he wore nothing to show allegiance to any realm, though I suspected him to be Karahsek. It was the way he spoke certain words.

Well, they took him and set fire to our ship. Strangely, they did what they said they would: they let us go. I don't know why, really. Considering the stories, It's out of character for her. Maybe she thought we didn't stand a chance in the skiff out on the open sea. I can't be sure. You know [nervous laughter] we all thought we were dead.

Anyway, we climbed into the skiff, lowered it into the water, and took to the oars as hard as we could. When our ship sank, we were alone on the sea. The *Sceptre of Night* had disappeared, as if she were never there.

And what happened after that?

We somehow made it back to Tava. When we beached the skiff the First Mate turned to me and said, "Looks like you'll have something interesting to write about."

SIXTEEN

–From the narrative by Rainer Eicher

Cutting the *Sceptre*'s engine, the sun-sails billowed in the night wind. The value of her ship—and to some extent her life—took on a more menacing importance. Kerrod was not simply her employer, engaged in the illicit trading of weapons. At least not anymore. The attack on the Karahsek ship, and the way he left them to die, was proof of that.

Setting the wheel, she tried to sleep on the cold deck. Tevis had relieved Kilso at the bow just after midnight. Kerrod remained below, with Rymah.

He had done a thorough job of keeping them apart.

She leaned back against the wheel mount. Above, the stars were glittering ice crystals, and the sea wind was a cold caress.

"Mistress Captain."

"Selasi?" She lifted her head. "What are you doing up here? And keep your voice down." She pointed to the bow. The boy spotted Tevis and nodded.

"I cannot sleep." He walked over and sat down next to her. "I think you cannot sleep, either."

She rubbed a palm across her face. "Sleep has not come easily for some time."

"You are troubled."

"I am, indeed."

"Mistress?"

"There are plans, Selasi, and plans within plans."

He titled his head. "I do not follow you, Mistress."

"Come on, Selasi, the keen observer." She patted his head. "I think you do. Think back on what happened the other day, with the Karahsek. Did anything strike you as out of the ordinary? Speak freely."

He bit his bottom lip, remembering. Then his eyes lit up. "The flags Kerrod used," he said. "I did not recognize their patterns. Must have been some type of code."

"Good. And?"

"The way they come alongside?" he said. "It was as though they were allies." He looked puzzled. "But if he is working with the Karahsek, then why kill them?"

"That's another thing that troubles me." Dema jumped at the flicker of a shadow. Rymah appeared and kneeled by her side.

Dema almost spoke Rymah's name too loudly but stopped herself and looked nervously at Tevis. He remained at the bow, unmoving, his back to them. Dema gripped Rymah with both hands. It took all her strength to let Rymah go.

"Are you okay?" Dema asked.

Kerrod. Not touch me.

Rymah reached out and stroked back Dema's sodden hair. Her caress was so enticing, so heartfelt, all Dema wanted at the moment was to drown in her.

I wish, Dema signed, *there was some part of your strangeness you could use against Kerrod.*

Rymah shook her head. *I do not kill.*

Dema collected her thoughts. *The artefact in the satchel. Can you tell me what it is?*

Rymah's face contorted, as if she were overcome with pain.

Have you seen it?

Rymah nodded. *Some things are better left to the sea.*

What's in the satchel? And why would he signal and then attack a Karahsek ship?

Rymah signed a response. Dema sat back against the wheel mount.

"Mistress," said the boy. "What is it?"

"Rymah says the artefact is a weapon."

"A weapon?"

"A weapon of the Anil," Dema said, and she thought about that.

"*That's* what Kerrod's been after?" Selasi said. "So there are there such things?"

"What do you know about machine artefacts?"

"Very little, Mistress. Although I was born on a ship, mid-voyage, I was raised in Tanpai."

She told him how no two artefacts sloughed from the machines were ever the same. Each one was an original, produced an original effect, and possessed a singular purpose.

"There is a story, perhaps you have not heard it," Dema said. "The Karahsek set off the first and only Anil weapon over two hundred years ago, by mistake. It took out an entire five-kilometre stretch of atolls to the southwest. To this day that part of the sea still glows in the dark."

Selasi's face dropped. "And they have been searching for another ever since."

Many have been looking, signed Rymah.

"And to find one," said Dema, "would make a nation the most powerful among all the island realms."

"Or the most dangerous. Seems Karahsek persistence has paid off, Mistress."

"So has Officer Kerrod's."

Selasi looked over his shoulder at Tevis, still sitting in the bow, then the boy turned to Rymah. "But what type of weapon could this be? And what kind of power could it yield?"

For the first time since Dema had known her, she thought Rymah looked genuinely terrified.

Rymah, Dema signed, *I must know Kerrod's next move. It appears he has betrayed his Karahsek allies. Will he give it to the Regent?*

Kerrod has no allies, she signed. *It will be sold. To the highest bidder.*

Dema went pale, quiet. Water broke against the sides of the ship with the sound of electric static.

"Mistress?"

"Selasi," she said. "Kerrod is going to sell it to whoever can pay his price."

They exchanged glances.

"Plans within plans," Selasi repeated her words.

"Exactly," Dema said.

"The Regent, then, knows nothing of this deception."

"And that means Kerrod had help from a source unknown to me as of yet." She thought about this. "And then there's the damned Karahsek."

"A traitor," Selasi said wildly. "He would conspire against his allies, and his own people…"

"He is not the first," she said. "We now know he runs weapons to mercenaries, pirates, maybe even an island authority or two, but small, distant quasi-nations on the fringes, further than Tanpai—"

"Loose associations," said Selasi, "like the smaller islands we have visited across the equator.

Disorganised, fighting amongst themselves."

"Exactly. Places so far away and so chaotic they would not draw any unwanted attention." Her enthusiasm for the topic grew, and she allowed herself to be swept up in it. "Let's say the Karahsek found out what he was doing. Not that they would care; raiding, embezzlement and war are the pillars of Karahsek life."

"And as he seems to be an expert at acquiring things," Selasi said, "they made him an offer, to work for them."

"Or so they thought."

Selasi hesitated, and thoughts gathered on his brow. "Are we so sure this is what has happened?"

Dema shrugged. "No. But it's as good a guess as any. What we do know is he signalled a Karahsek ship, they came alongside, he stole what they had and murdered them."

"And if Rymah is right about the artefact…"

"When it comes to artefacts, Rymah is always right."

"Then I suspect, Mistress, he will need a J'Niah to help him figure out how to operate it."

"Not Rymah. I won't allow them to use her."

The boy suddenly looked ill. "And she says Kerrod is going to sell this weapon."

Dema shook her head. "Not if I get it first."

"And throw it into the sea, I hope," Selasi said.

"No." Dema's face was stern, and a hard line was drawn across her brow. "It's an opportunity. To clear my name."

"How so, Mistress?"

Dema's eyes were distant. The Assembly of the Three Realms, which included Quiru, the Confederacy and the Nawa'i Atoll, had kept their shipping routes

Karahsek free for many years. But if the Assembly wanted to expand its reach, they would need to get rid of the Karahsek threat. She could provide the means for them, for a price.

"If I bring this weapon to the Assembly," she said, "explain what has happened, maybe they'll drop the charges against me."

The boy's face lit up. "By the Temple of Erdi, they might!"

"You, Selasi, can bear witness. And Rymah," Dema said, "we'll have enough wealth to buy a fleet of ships. We may even find your fabled city."

Rymah became visibly distressed, covered her mouth with both hands, and backed away. As Dema and Selasi turned to see what frightened her a shadow fell upon them both.

Tevis stood over them. "What you're more likely to find is a hole in your head." He took out his pistol and pushed the end of the barrel into the side of her skull. "Get up, Mistress Captain!"

She got to her feet. Tevis grabbed her arm.

"You, boy," he said, "will take the J'Niah below and stay there. Wake Kerrod and tell him—"

In one quick motion Dema yanked her arm free and drove her elbow up into his gullet, cutting off his windpipe. He dropped the gun, gasping, and his hands flew up to his throat. Dema caught the weapon before it hit the deck. She then drew herself up, held the gun over her head, and brought it crashing down upon his skull. She caught him as he collapsed and lay him across a sail locker.

"Mistress," said the boy. "What are you going to do?"

"An opportunity has presented itself," she said. "Now's our chance."

"To retake the ship?"

"No. One of us would get killed, for sure. Rymah will get the artefact, and the three of us will take our chances in the lifepod."

Rymah stiffened and drew a defiant line across her chest with a hand. *No!*

We can do it! Dema signed.

Rymah tried to sign but let her hands collapse into her lap.

"Three in a lifepod," Selasi screwed up his face. "A tight squeeze."

"I'll destroy the batteries at the stern, so they cannot make or receive transmissions. And that'll effectively kill the engines, too. When we are far enough away, I'll hit the lifepod's distress beacon."

"They'll still have the sails."

"True. But we'll keep the pod lights off. In the dark they won't be able to find us. And the pod's motor has a single battery with a four-hour charge. I'll pour all the juice into it. That should put enough distance between us and this ship."

"We'll no doubt hit a current," said Selasi, "and that will carry us further out."

Dema nodded. "It'll be dangerous."

"Better than staying here. As I said before, I am with you, Mistress." The boy let out a small laugh. "Surprised we did not think of this plan sooner."

"We lacked the proper motivation."

"The artefact," Selasi said.

"Yes. And what that weapon means for me now." She

looked to Rymah. "What it means for us." She signed: *We've been near death before and come out the other side. Trust me, as you've done many times before.*

This is not about trust. It's about what is possible.

"Only you can go below and get the artefact. I'm not allowed below deck. If he wakes and finds me down there where I don't belong our chance is certainly ruined…"

Rymah remained defiant. She balled up one fist and shook her head.

Dema stood confused at her sudden dissent.

Selasi shook her arm. "Mistress?"

"Get into the pod. Check the provisions, under the seats."

The boy moved toward the pod, hanging off the rear starboard quarter of the ship.

"We don't have time to argue, Rymah," she said. "My life depends on it, as well as the boy's. And so does yours." Dema bent down in front of the wheel mount and pulled open the service hatch. It would drop Rymah into the engine shaft, behind the hold and crew quarters. "You must help me clear my name."

Rymah took a step back, arms behind her. A sign she no longer wished to speak.

"Rymah—" Her voice was stopped by the sound of the pump action of a rifle.

"Lower the hatch." Kilso was halfway out of the crew hatch, mid-ship. He stepped aside and Kerrod came up on deck. Dema let the hatch go. It slammed shut.

Kerrod looked around, then set his eyes on the pod. "Come out of there, boy!"

Selasi emerged from the pod, slowly, and came

toward Kerrod. He raised his hands and placed them behind his head.

Kilso pointed aft. "Over there. It's Tevis."

"He'd better be alive," said Kerrod.

Kilso ran to the slumped body on the sail locker. He bent down and put an ear to the man's chest. After a few seconds he stood back up. "He lives."

Kerrod walked toward Dema with purpose and backhanded her, hard. She crashed against the wheel mount. Blood filled her mouth. She turned her head and spat it at him, spraying the right side of his face.

He stood glaring at her, while the blood ran down to his neck in small rivulets. Without moving his eyes from Dema he pointed at Rymah. "Get below," he said, voice cold and measured.

Rymah hesitated, made a crude gesture, and left the deck.

Dema raised an eyebrow. "Never seen her say that before. 'Son of a whore.' Well, she's got you pegged."

He took out his pistol. "If you try something like that again" —he pointed the gun at the boy's head— "I'll kill him."

Selasi blanched in terror.

"Kerrod, he's just a boy."

He shrugged. "The boy is the only one I can kill. For the moment." He holstered his weapon. "Remember that."

Kilso helped a semi-conscious Tevis get below. Kerrod sat in the bow.

Dawn now broke upon a grey sea.

The boy stood silently by her side.

"Selasi," she said after some time, "I would not have allowed him to harm you. Believe that."

"I believe you, Mistress," he uttered. "And you were right, with Kerrod I had no choice. I was an instrument to secure you here, with the promise of a great adventure to tell."

"Once again, you torment yourself. I said I understood. Now let it go."

Selasi looked up at her.

"I am not here to write his story, or anyone else's. Am I?"

She sighed and shook her head.

"I was wrong, Mistress. Rymah is not the guarantor on this ship, is she?"

"No, young Selasi, the Good Bard," she said, placing a hand upon his shoulder. "You are."

SEVENTEEN

–From the annals of Avram Aul

Alert: A Severn Islands Priority Broadcast.

Be on the lookout for the *Sceptre of Night*, formerly the *Wave Rider*. STOP. Last seen heading northeast, near Devlin's Rock. STOP. Raided service station on the Kai Cay. STOP. Killed all six servicemen, stole supplies. STOP. The Nawa'i ship *Mastersinger* in pursuit. STOP. All available ships within the vicinity to respond. STOP. Co-ordinates to follow.

This has been a Severn Islands Priority Broadcast.
End Transmission.

EIGHTEEN

–From the narrative by Rainer Eicher

Dema was busy altering their course to avoid an approaching storm when Kerrod appeared. "Stay your course," he said. "North-by-northeast. There's a field of sea-stalks not far from here. That's our destination."

"That's into the storm," Dema protested. "Without good visibility and accurate charts, I can't plot a safe course. I can't use the device, either. We might crash into something."

"Stay your course."

Dema lit the chemical hurricane lamp and ran it up the mainsail. The waves began to grow, surging across the sea like angry fists. It began to rain.

Selasi, as ever, stood by her side.

"Mistress," he said, "you cannot steer us into that storm. We will never make it."

"Seems I have little choice." She looked towards the bow where Kerrod now stood. He turned and locked eyes with her. "He'll get us out of this somehow," she said, "or he wouldn't being doing it."

Selasi sneered. "You mean he will get himself out of this."

"He's not finished with us yet. But when he is, he may want you alive after all, to write his story. Whoever he sells the artefact to will make him a wealthy man and a hero of their realm."

"Some story." Selasi spit on the deck. "I will not write it."

She shrugged. "It's the one he wants for himself."

"He should have thought of that before using me to trap you, and then as his guarantor…"

She smiled and nudged him. "I want you to get below. No protest, young Selasi."

"But Mistress…"

"When that storm hits, I don't want you thrown overboard. Besides, there'll be a machine field nearby. Keep an eye on Rymah for me. If those machines show signs of an imminent discharge, charts or no charts, and whether Kerrod likes it or not, I'm going to risk hitting the displacement device."

The boy relented and went below.

After several hours the tall shapes of the machines eventually seeped through the wall of grey rain, ominous and very close; their stalks pierced the low ceiling of cloud. The wind rumbled in her ears.

"Keep her steady." Kerrod moved mid-ship. Dema noticed Tevis and Kilso had taken up their usual positions.

Another raid? she thought. For what purpose? He now had what he wanted.

"What are we doing here?" she said.

Kerrod said nothing.

"The boy will tell us if those machines are going to discharge."

"No need," said Kerrod. "These particular machines haven't discharged in over a hundred years."

"These are The Silent Ones!" she whispered to herself. She tried to ascertain their position from memory: Three days past Devlin's Rock, turn due north…

At the base of the nearest machine the outline of a ship rose up to run parallel with the *Sceptre*. Its shape and muted colours became clear as the gap closed between them.

Dema's ears burned with fear and outrage.

It was the *Godsong*. Captain Ogunwe was leaning over the starboard side, one hand gripping the ratlines.

She turned on Kerrod and cursed him.

Kerrod smiled, "My only regret is that I won't be the one to kill you." He pulled out a pistol. "Keep your hands away from that device. Lock the wheel and step away."

She did as she was told.

The *Godsong* pulled alongside. Two ropes were thrown across. Tevis and Kilso ran to secure them. The ships were close enough for Ogunwe and two men to jump aboard. They flanked Kerrod, who kept his pistol aimed at her.

"Dema Ägan," said Ogunwe above the din. "It's good to see you again."

One of Ogunwe's men suddenly pivoted, rifle raised. Two thunder cracks sounded. Tevis and Kilso crumpled to the rain-soaked deck.

Kerrod spun around, eyes wide. Ogunwe pulled a long blade from under his belt and thrust it up under Kerrod's chin and into his skull. He twitched a moment, then Ogunwe shoved him overboard.

"No allies. No witnesses," Dema said. "That's how you play it, hey, Captain Ogunwe?"

"Always."

"Kerrod was a high-ranking official who came with connections to make this campaign a success, but I see now he was never really in charge. And Captain Meloy?"

He grinned. "Meloy was a fool and easily led. He did what he was told, mostly. Kerrod's vanity made it easy to make him believe he was in charge and had the upper hand."

"Any more in this little network of yours?"

"As for others I've had the pleasure of working with, well…" He shrugged.

"Many hands make a job easier," Dema said.

He held up a finger. "But not too many. One or two here or there. Just enough to be of assistance."

"And then eliminated."

"Of course. And some even had J'Niahs." He grinned again and barked over his shoulder: "Gad, secure the *Sceptre* for towing. Omah, fetch the weapon. And bring up the J'Niah. Be quick!"

Omah went below and returned with the satchel, leading Rymah by the arm. The boy followed, clutching his book under his overcoat. Omah left them both with Ogunwe and jumped back across to the *Godsong*.

"Take the boy with you," she said.

"But of course," he replied in mock horror. "Do you think I am a killer of children?" He spoke over his shoulder: "Get aboard, boy."

Selasi remained rooted where he stood. "Mistress, no!"

"Go," Dema said. "Now!"

"Unless you want to die here," added Ogunwe. "I offer you protection this one time, boy. I suggest you take it."

Dema nodded to Selasi. "Go. It's okay."

"But Mistress…"

"It's okay."

Selasi stood for a moment, eyes brimming with tears, then he leapt aboard the *Godsong*.

"I will leave him at the next available port," Ogunwe said. "An inconspicuous port, of course. He can make his way home from there. Satisfied?"

"I am. And what of Rymah?"

Ogunwe looked at the J'Niah and smiled.

Dema was about to sign when she noticed the ease at which Rymah was standing. Rymah looked at Ogunwe for what seemed to be an eternity before casting her gaze to Dema.

And with that Dema knew. She *knew*. Sailing the Great Storm Season, outrunning black ships, attempting to navigate the pole, only to be thwarted by ice sheets and making their own warmth below deck, waiting for the seasons to turn and the routes to open again—all those moments that defined them and secured their love fell away.

Dema let out an anguished wail.

Dema, Rymah signed. *I need*.

"When did you two…" Dema said. "How long have you been…"

"Long enough," said Ogunwe.

"Gods, Rymah, what did he promise you? That he knows the location of Anua? That he can take you there?"

Understand. I need. Anua. Rymah banged her fist against her chest. *Understand.*

"I've nearly died for you! I've begged, stolen—" Tears gathered in her eyes. "I did it for us. But there is no us, is there? There is only you! Meloy found that out—"

Anua. He give. She signed with a bold certainty.

"Fight your blind instinct! Think with your intellect. Ogunwe set us both up! He has the *Sceptre* now. And the weapon. Rymah, my foolish love, do you know what you've done?"

Anua. He give!

"He needs you to figure out how that weapon works. Then he'll kill you. You'll never see Anua!"

Rymah stepped back, as slowly as the surging deck would allow. *I need. Understand.*

Gad came forward. "Secured. But we must go. The storm is gathering strength."

"So it is," said Ogunwe. "Lock our dear Mistress Captain in the hold."

Gad grinned. "It'll be a long journey. She'll provide an ample distraction."

"I'll kill the first man or woman who touches me," Dema snarled. "I promise you."

Ogunwe laughed. "Mistress Captain, I would not permit such a thing to happen, no matter what Gad, here, says. Unlike some of my crew, I am not an animal."

"How reassuring."

"Be assured that I will kill you," he said. "But not today. I may still have need of you. For what purpose, that is what I have to think on." He motioned to Gad. "Take our daring Mistress Captain aboard."

"Aye."

Ogunwe took Rymah by the arm. "This ship made you an exceptional opponent, Dema Ägan. But without it, you're nothing."

And with that Ogunwe and Rymah jumped to the *Godsong*. Dema watched, helplessly, as a crewman ushered Rymah below.

Gad came and grabbed Dema's arm. He clapped an iron cuff around her wrist and held firmly to the chain. Rain lashed her face. The deck pitched in the boiling sea and a wave crashed across the stern.

"No," she uttered, then gritted her teeth and growled: "*No!*" She yanked back on the chain, throwing Gad off balance. He'd let enough of the chain go to create some slack. Dema whipped it over his head, around his neck, and pulled. His neck snapped. The chain clattered to the decking.

The boy's voice came crashing through the storm: "*Mistress!*"

Dema turned to see Ogunwe on the deck of the *Godsong*, reaching for the rifle on his back. Pulling the pistol from Gad's holster she swung round wildly, yelled, "Down, boy!" and as he disappeared below the side railing, she fired multiple shots, sending Ogunwe and his crew diving for cover.

She aimed high, up the *Sceptre*'s mainmast, and fired steadily, shredding the lines and braces. The topsail collapsed and the hurricane lamp plummeted down. It crashed into a sail locker and exploded. Flames shot up, grabbed at the rigging and the flapping sails.

While the flames provided some cover, she discarded the empty cartridge, pulled another from Gad's belt, and locked it in place. Turning quickly, she aimed for a spot of decking behind the *Sceptre*'s wheel and fired relentlessly, shredding the engine's battery covering. The ship dipped, and another wave came crashing over the stern, soaking the cells. The exposed vitriol surged and frothed, releasing clouds of yellow-green gas which rose up and tumbled across the decks of both ships. Ogunwe and his men fell back from the choking fumes.

Tossing the empty gun away, Dema made for the *Sceptre*'s starboard side and jumped into the lifepod, pulling the wrist-chain in behind her in one rapid motion. The pod's automation was quick, and as the plastic covering slammed shut the explosive bolts ignited, releasing the craft. The pod fell away into the sea amid the roar of gunfire.

The rolling waves, higher, more rapid now, swiftly carried the pod off into the blanket of grey. Through the rain she could see the *Godsong*'s crew, axes in hand, frantically cutting the tow lines, releasing the burning *Sceptre* to the depths.

And as the rain beat down and the waves thundered, she wrapped her arms around herself and cried, shaking with the bitterness of revelation. She cared neither for the compass, nor for the direction in which the sea was taking her.

As she watched the silhouette of the *Godsong* vanish into the storm she whispered fervently, "Rymah. You fool! *Oh, you fool!*"

Reaching into her tunic she took out the pendant that hung low about her neck, the one Rymah had given her, an artefact smooth and cool and alien.

Dema stared at it through burning tears, looked at it with a desperate hope, willing the sparks to ignite, climb into the air and dance. And she thought if she looked hard enough, those sparks might grow into shards, and the shards come together, and an image would rise up from her palm, exotic and brilliant.

A magnificent city of light.

of burning tears and bright water

The sun has long since come up from under the ocean and sits on the edge of the far horizon, and the sea outside the window is now a field of jewels, glistening in the hard light of morning, clear, bright. The only sound is the gentle shush of the surf against the rocks and sand below.

I find the Director standing on a balcony. I step carefully through the open glass doors and take my place next to him. He does not turn to me but keeps his eyes thrown outward, squinting into the morning's blazing light, as if longing for what might lie beyond that horizon.

When he does look at me his eyes take in every aspect of my face, as though recognizing something there. He nods to himself, satisfied by what he sees.

"You have come a long way I take it," he says, "through many years. Did you find what you were looking for?"

My chest tightens, constricting with emotions I had thought long dead. And I see her face, Dema's face, young, weary, as it was all those years ago; I see the cuts and scratches on her bare arms, the bruises on her bare thighs, and the blood that dried there. I see her now at the cupboard, hand reaching in and drawing out what money is there. She sees me now, watching her from the bedroom door. She smiles faintly and tries to tell me with her lonely eyes that all will be okay. I see her wrap her coat about her shoulders and slip out into the bitter, northern night.

I feel the crushing weight of that moment once again.

He turns his eyes back toward the horizon and the rising sun. "Ogunwe did not expect to find her aboard *The Moira*; he did not expect her to survive when he burned it down. After, when Rymah learned that Dema still lived, I suspect she convinced Ogunwe of Dema's usefulness."

"The murder charge got in the way."

He nods. "But fate arrived in the guise of Tove Garbarek. She unintentionally did the hard work for them when she arranged for Dema's escape from Quiru."

"The navigator?"

"He was merely there by chance. There is little information on him. He was not a man of these islands, but he was a man who had a reason to leave, and quickly."

I consider his words.

"Garbarek never came back to these parts," I say.

"No. She was killed some years later, in a Karahsek raid."

The surf is a pulsating rhythm of static.

"And Rymah?"

He closes his eyes, as if in great pain.

"J'Niahs do not do anything by accident." The Director's head swivels slowly, and his eyes grip mine. "They are driven, you see, by a fierce sense of survival, and a desperate need to reach a place that may or may not exist."

"And at any cost," I say. I think about this. "Seems like she was hedging her bets, this Rymah, keeping her options open. Dema or Ogunwe."

He leans forward slightly, eyes glossy, wet. A profound sadness falls upon him.

"It was the worst kind of betrayal," he says. "Dema was loyal to her, loved her. But when it became clear to Rymah that Dema would never really get her to Anua, and that Dema had lost to Ogunwe—"

It is my turn to look toward the blazing horizon.

"Dema never had a chance," I mutter. "Crossing sea after sea, learning how to run a ship, to be a mariner, becoming a mariner of some stature, and to lose it all in such a way…"

"So, you understand?"

I swallow. "I've spent my whole life hating her, for leaving us behind. For leaving me. Stuck there on that northern shore, enduring that man, until I was old enough to make my own escape." I feel tears well-up in my eyes, a few drops run down my face. "Dema Ägan." I laugh and shake my head. "It's an anagram for our mother's name, Megan Däan. After mother and father died from the disease and we were rehoused, she used to make up stories to tell us little ones. She would use names of family members, mix the letters about to come up with characters. She loved telling stories of Dema Ägan the most: Dema the Mariner, the hero of the seas…" I shake my head again.

"And when you came across the name in your journeys…"

I nod. "Of course, I knew it was her, and that she must be around, somewhere. So, I set about searching.

And the accusations of murder and piracy served to fuel the vile image I'd created of her in my mind."

The morning breeze whispers between us. Out on the water, the glint of a sun-sail holds my attention for a moment. I watch it move gracefully toward the harbour.

"She was a child," he says, "carrying a heavy burden. She was anguished. At the time, running away was the only option available to her." His gaze turns inward and a shadow passes across his face.

Fluid rises in my throat. I swallow the bile of those northern days and shake my head, as though trying to fling the memories off my skull.

The Director lifts his eyes to look at me again. "She could not stay, you understand. But believe me when I say, leaving you—all of you—still haunted her down the long years."

The hairs on the back on my neck stand up in a cold moment of revelation.

"You're the boy," I say. "You're Selasi!"

He smiles, gently. "Yes, I am Selasi. And Rainer Eicher. I am both."

My mouth is open, but nothing comes out.

"Yes," he continues, "and I know who you are. At first, I was not sure, but later…"

"My accent."

"You did a decent job of trying to disguise it. You sound so much like her. When I look close enough, I swear I can see a part of her in your face, the way you move your head, even some of your mannerisms."

There is a moment of silence.

"She told me much during the short time I was with her." The Director's voice is thoughtful, almost sad.

"And I wrote down what I could. I thought to pass it off as a dramatic narrative because, at the time, it was easier to get it published and circulated."

"You felt responsible."

"Of course. And I was," he says. "I was part of Kerrod's plan to capture her. Despite that, she saved me from him, saved my life. I owed it to her to write what I could. Our stories are all we have, you see. Legends, rumours, those are lies that had defined her for so long. I wanted to compile her real story, as incomplete as that story may be. As incomplete as any of our stories are."

A seagull cries in the distance.

"And the weapon?" I ask. "Where is it now?"

"At the bottom of the sea. The storm raged on into the next day. Ogunwe's ship not only had a skiff but a lifepod as well, hanging off the stern. As the storm reached its height, I took my chance and escaped. Ogunwe survived, so I heard, but his ship and most of his crew were lost." He clears his throat. "As for Rymah, I never saw her again. There have been various sightings over the years, of course, but they always came to nothing."

"The pod carrying Dema—never found, I take it."

He clasps his hands together. "There are no records from any of the ships in that area at that time picking up a distress beacon."

We move back through the corridor, to the stacks of the Archives. Sunlight pours through the windows and the room is warm now. Both books are lying on the table. Eicher's book—the Director's book—is open, the last page splashed with golden light. I close the book with great care.

"I've been chasing rumours for so long," I say. "Now that it's over, I feel lost."

"Feeling lost is just an opportunity to strike out on a new course." The Director motions out the window. "Look at the sea. It stretches farther than any mariner has ever travelled and is deeper than anyone could ever know. Is it not time to make your own way?"

Across the harbor, the ships glitter on the water, tall and proud. Like Dema, I feel a stirring within, a stirring for winds and currents and far places.

I see her face again, her lonely eyes…

"Tell me, truthfully." I turn to him. "Do you think she lives?"

"Does anyone know for certain?" he says.

And I think I see, perched upon his lips, the shadow of a smile.

END

About the Author

Carmelo Rafala, a child of Sicilian immigrants, grew up in New England. As a student he travelled the world and somehow managed to finish his MA in Comparative Literature at the University of South Africa, as well as his MSC in Student Advice and Guidance at Central Connecticut State University. As an editor, he has worked with many writers in the the field of speculative fiction whose books have gone on to be nominated for several awards.

Carmelo's short stories have been published to much praise in various anthologies and magazines. His work has been translated into Romanian. He currently lives on the south coast of England where he is being held hostage by a large collection of books. If you are concerned for his welfare, send dark chocolate and a decent bottle of Scotch.

More great fantasy novellas from GUARDBRIDGE BOOKS.

The King of Next Week
by E. C. Ambrose

When a captain trades his cargo of ice to bring home a djinn bride, his life in coastal Maine will never be the same.

A Fledgeling Abiba
by Dilman Dila

An orphaned teenage girl tries to survive on her own and understand her magical powers while a sorcerous plague sweeps the country. She may hold the key to its cure, but what she really wants is somewhere she can call home and family.

Death by Effigy
A Novella of Mystery, Magic, and Marionettes in 19th Century Burma.
by Karen L. Abrahamson

A traditional Burmese puppetry troupe is more than meets the eye: these puppets hold living spirits.

Aung, the troupe's elderly singer, must navigate the labyrinth of court intrigues to solve a mystery and appease angry spirits—goals which might might be at odds.

Myriad Lands
Anthology of Multi-cultural and Non-traditional fantasy.

Beyond familiar tropes, there is a world of possibilities for fantasy literature. This 2 volume anthology contains stories from around our world and breathtaking fictional worlds.

Features stories by Tade Thompson, Mary Anne Mohanraj, Phenderson Djèlí Clark, Tanith Lee, Adrian Tchaikovsky, Walter Dinjos, and more.

All are available at our website and online retailers.
http://guardbridgebooks.co.uk

Lightning Source UK Ltd.
Milton Keynes UK
UKHW011506070720
366156UK00003B/644